UNDER THE HEMLOCK TREE

A COMING-OF-AGE STORY

AUBREY DELACETTE

EDITED BY
MICHELLE WHITE

Cover design by Silvana G. Sánchez © SP Designs www.selfpubdesigns.com

Edited by Michelle White, Divine Love Enterprises LLC, michelle@twinflamewarriors.com

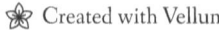 Created with Vellum

To my mentors for their love and encouraging words.

TRIGGER WARNING & DISCLAIMER

This book contains themes and/or descriptions of ABUSE, CHILDHOOD TRAUMA, DYSFUNCTIONAL FAMILIES & RELATIONSHIPS, MENTAL ILLNESS, NONTRADITIONAL GENDER RELATIONSHIPS, RELIGION, and SEXUAL VIOLENCE. If you are sensitive to this subject matter, please consider other content.

Under the Hemlock Tree is a work of fiction. This book does not provide factual health or mental health information or strategies. All names, characters, businesses, events, incidents, and language are the products of the author's imagination or used in an exclusively fictitious manner. Any resemblance to actual persons, living or dead, is unintended and purely coincidental.

The content of *Under the Hemlock Tree* is exclusively designed for entertainment purposes and is not intended to diagnose, treat, cure, or prevent any condition or disease which may be portrayed or implied in its narrative. This book is not intended as a substitute for consultation with a licensed practitioner. Please consult a physician or health-care specialist if you require further information regarding issues described in this fictional book.

PART ONE

CHAPTER 1
FALL
CHELSEA

August

watched out the window as my bus rolled up to the desolate junction of two dusty county roads. I didn't expect anyone to be waiting to greet me after school, and I wasn't disappointed. When the brakes squealed, I grabbed my backpack and three-ring binder before sliding to the edge of the slippery green vinyl seat. A boy's voice rang out from the far back of the bus.

"White trash walking!" Two other boys laughed. I turned to seek out their faces. They tried to mask their laughter, but they couldn't control themselves. Typical. I shot daggers at them with my eyes, mustering all the hatred I felt for them, everyone at school, and this backwater hell-hole I couldn't wait to escape.

"Skanky ho," someone else joined the banter.

"Look, she's trying to put on her ratty backpack. That's not happening," the first boy snickered. He was right. I couldn't zip it because it was brimming with text-books. I slipped one strap over my shoulder and eased into the walkway. The chorus of boys kept jawing at my expense.

"I'm going to cop a feel when she walks past. Watch me," one commented. Everyone laughed, including the girls. I glimpsed the driver in the backward-facing observation mirror, trying to stifle his amusement. So much for trusted adults. Visions of school shooters swirled in my mind as I walked what felt like a mile down the bus's center aisle. Were they as viciously ridiculed every hour, day, week, month, and year as I had been, I wondered?

I arrived beside the driver. He swung open the door. Head held high, I stepped down, eager to escape the nause-ating sideshow my so-called Christian classmates forced me to star in. On the second riser, I lost my balance, landed on my knees on the sharp metal edge of the step, and fell flat on the dirt road.

"Oh my gosh, her skankiness fell," a girl leaned out of a window and twisted her head to relay a play-by-play of my humiliation to the audience inside the yellow metal tube that served as a circus tent. I lay in a heap where I'd fallen, clothing in disarray. The driver spoke, but I couldn't hear him over the laughter. "I don't know why they let someone like *that* into our school," the commentator concluded, drawing her head back inside.

Pain radiated down my legs. When I pushed myself up to test whether they'd hold me, my books spilled out of my pack, flopping like dead fish on the road. The three-ring binder snapped open and relinquished its papers to the breeze. I watched them disperse across the farm field adja-cent to the road. *Don't cry, Chelsea,* I warned myself. *Hang on tight! Don't ever let them see you cry.*

"Are you done with your gymnastics? I have a schedule to keep," steamed the driver.

"Wait! I forgot a book," I climbed back aboard the SS Freakshow and retraced my steps. I stopped beside the seat I'd vacated and faced my tormentors. I stood straight and tall, willing my full figure to fill the space between the green vinyl seats, drawing all eyes to me.

"Your attention, please. I have an important announcement," I said with authority. The bus fell silent. All my life, I'd endured insults. I was done taking what was dished out. "Will the Christian boys in the back please raise their hands?" No one did. "Thank you for your honesty," I said sarcastically. They looked confused. "Listen up, now," I maintained my authoritative tone. "GO FUCK YOURSELVES!"

"Chelsea!" yelled the bus driver. I ignored him.

"Here I have one of God's little creatures for you," I turned in a slow circle, flipping the entire bus the bird. "Fuck with me again, and I'll kick your ever-loving mother's asses."

"If only you had an ever-loving mother," someone mocked. A new symphony of insults arose around me.

"Her mother's crazy. Certifiable, my mom says."

"Like mother, like daughter. Psycho!"

I'd had enough. I genuflected on a bloody knee and crossed myself.

"I have a gift for you, fake Christian sinners. I hereby lay a permanent curse," I raised my arms high as if imploring God. "May you all get cancer and rot in hell for eternity!" Everyone stared at me open-mouthed. You could've heard a pin drop.

"CHELSEA," the bus driver bellowed. "No foul language on my bus! You are well aware that I have a *zero-*

tolerance policy for curse words," I saw a few kids mouthing the words in sync with him. "Do I have to report you to the Chaplain?"

I lowered my arms, turned, and shouted back at him, "Why don't you report the cock-sucking bullies?"

"Whoa," someone in the audience breathed. The bus driver blinked in the observation mirror.

"Cool it, Chelsea," I watched him regain his fake Christian calm. "Please get off my bus," he said, "and watch your tongue. One more outburst and I'll report you to the Chaplain without a second thought."

The last thing you need is to get kicked out your senior year because of these assholes, I cautioned myself. I got off the bus.

As I surveyed the paper-strewn landscape, someone stepped down to join me on the gravel road. Usually, I was the only one who used this stop. I replayed the laying-of-the-curse scene in my mind, recalling an unfamiliar student who sat in the front seat, observing the pandemonium without contributing. I studied this person, who stood beside me, trying to tell whether it was a boy or a girl. The bus pulled away in a puff of exhaust as the stranger knelt to gather my books.

"You're bleeding," it pointed to my legs and looked up at me through rich chocolate-brown eyes. I followed its finger to my knees, which looked like ground meat. My eyes flicked back to its face. The delicate features, petite figure, and long brown ponytail spoke of a female. But the rough voice sounded like a male's. It crab-walked to my side, pulled a handkerchief from the pocket of its pants, and pressed the linen square against the raw mess. I flinched in agony.

"Quit staring up my dress," I growled, instinctively

clutching one arm across my chest. With the other hand, I gathered the pleated folds of my skirt and squeezed the fabric tight around my thighs.

"You need stitches," said the stranger calmly.

"What the fuck are you? A Good Samaritan? Or a pervert?"

"Neither."

"Get away from me," I backed up a step.

"Do they always treat you like that?" The concern didn't sound fake. I lost control and started to cry.

"Leave me alone," I turned to hobble home, abandoning my possessions to their fate. It was a half-mile walk to the house I lived in with my mom and dad. The pain in my knees was so intense that I could hardly bend them. *Stop crying,* I told myself every other step. It became a chant in my head. *Stop crying. Don't feel. Stop crying. Don't feel.*

Halfway home, I heard footsteps. I whirled around. The stranger was ten feet behind me, both shoulders weighed down by backpacks and both arms stacked with binders and books.

"Why are you following me?"

"I have your things," the pest stepped in my direction.

"Don't come any closer," I ordered. "Throw my stuff right there on the ground!"

"I can carry it home for you. I don't mind."

"Who do you think you are?"

"A Good Samaritan," it shrugged, amusement etched on its pretty face. The books wobbled.

"Don't rub my nose in your Christian morality," I snapped. "Not while the spawn of Satan on that bus is allowed to spew its evil filth unchecked!"

With a lopsided grin, the stranger steadied the load and said conversationally, "They're pathetic excuses for Christians, aren't they? Who would think it could happen at a good parochial school like ours? Outrageous!" I was about to tell it to go away again, but it continued, "Look, there's nothing to be suspicious of. I'm showing you the same courtesy I'd show any male, female, or anyone in between. I promise I won't hurt you." In my head, something clicked. Everyone at school was talking about the rise of the LGBT community as if it was some big scandal. There were even a few parent complaints last year when our social studies teacher taught a unit about the battle over same-sex marriage in California. Maybe this was one of them.

"You couldn't hurt me if you tried. Do, and I'll kick your bony little ass," I sneered. "Bring me my things." The stranger approached. It held out my stack of books. I promptly dropped them when they slid onto my arm. In perfect sync, my half-open backpack hopped off the stranger's shoulder. A gust of wind whisked what remained of my homework across the road.

"Don't worry, I've got it," my companion sprang into action, loping after the fluttering papers.

"Stop," I yelled. "I don't need your help!" The wind swept a page away just as the kid bent down to pick it up. Watching the retrieval operation, I remembered last spring. During a solitary walk around our remote area, I came upon a bulldozer clearing a new private drive. After dinner one evening, I ignored the 'do not trespass' signs and ambled down the driveway, a quarter mile through a field and into a white oak woodlot. Along a creek, I spotted a new modern mansion. No one was around. I approached the construction site. Inside, I wandered through a large walk-in basement, then climbed the stairs. On the main floor, I found the primary bedroom. The suite included a vast space for a king-size bed, three walk-in closets, and a dressing room.

The bathroom featured two sinks, two toilets, and a hot tub. I opened the glass door to the walk-in shower and sat on a long stone bench. Although I was within a half-mile of my home, I felt I was in another country.

"Hello? Chelsea?" the stranger waved a hand in my face, and the memory faded. I focused on its face. Boy? Girl? I was still uncertain.

"You didn't have to do that," I said rudely, grabbing my things from its outstretched arms.

"I know I didn't have to. I wanted to."

"Whatever. I'm not going to thank you. I didn't ask for your help," I spun on my heel and limped away with as much dignity as I could muster.

It took another half-hour to get home and up the front steps. I stumped inside, kicked off my shoes, and threw down my school things. Under the harsh bathroom light, I shimmied out of my skirt. Bright red blood smeared the waistband. *Fucking figures it'd get on my clothes,* I thought. *Guess I'm doing laundry tonight.*

"Chelsea, are you home?" called my mother. Her muffled voice revealed she was closeted behind her bedroom door, as usual.

"Yes, Mom," I called back. "I scraped my knees getting off the bus. I'll come to say hi once I clean them." Finding that no washcloths or towels were laid out, I rummaged under the sink. "Guess I'm doing towels tonight, too," I muttered. Sitting on the edge of the tub, I unbuttoned and shrugged off my white blouse, which I used to dab at my bloody knee. When the bleeding slowed to a trickle, I pitched the stained garment on top of the overflowing hamper. I snapped off the bathroom light.

Walking down the hall, I saw I'd left the front door partially open. I went to close it and discovered the stranger lurking in the doorway. After the initial shock, my first thought was to cover myself up, but I couldn't care less who saw me today.

"What the hell are you doing here?" I stood straight and unflinching.

"I wanted to make sure you got home safely, and I collected these along the road," it held up a handful of soiled papers.

"Who's at the door?" called my mother.

"No one, Mom!"

"Who are you talking to? I hear a man's voice. Chelsea, tell him to go away."

"I got this, Mom," I reached out a hand and pushed the pest squarely in its flat chest. It stumbled backward onto the front porch. Despite wearing only my bra and panties, I stepped boldly outside and closed the door behind me. "You need to leave. You're upsetting my mother."

"I'm sorry. That wasn't my intention. I'd be happy to come in and meet her."

I narrowed my eyes and said, "Didn't anyone tell you? No one comes into our house."

"No one's said anything to me about you."

"You're lying," I accused, surprised that the newcomer's family hadn't been warned about us.

"I don't lie. I'm not a fake Christian like the others."

"Just a Good Samaritan, right?" I snorted.

Perfectly serious, my visitor replied, "I believe in God, and I try to follow in Jesus' footsteps. But I can't claim to be a righteous Samaritan."

"Well, there's no room for you, Jesus, or God in this house. Think of it as a nuclear dump site," I crossed my arms over my chest.

"What should I do with your papers? If you need help cleaning them up, I can do that."

"Just give them to me," I uncrossed my arms and held out a hand. My visitor hesitated. "Unless you're afraid to get too close to a half-naked girl," I mocked.

Finally, a reaction!

"You're blushing," I gloated. "You've never seen a girl in her underwear?" No answer. I stepped forward and grabbed the papers. The kid gulped and looked away from my face, first to one side, then the other. Then, downward. I waited. A moment passed as this person I was starting to suspect was a boy stared at my breasts, my waist, my legs.

"I, uh," it stammered. "Blood's dripping down your shins again. I took a first aid course over the summer. I can wash and bandage your cuts."

"Are you a moron? Try touching me again, and I'll plant my foot in your pretty little face."

"Why won't you let me help you?" the pretty little face searched mine.

"I don't want your help or pity," I glared. "Don't ever speak to me again. Now, get the hell off of my property and never come back."

"Your knees are in terrible shape," it insisted. "I think you need to see a doctor." Fed up and frustrated, I reached back and slapped the perfect face.

"Quit harassing me, you skinny little bitch!" I shrieked.

"You don't need to get violent," the stunned visitor rubbed its cheek. "You don't need to insult me, either. If that's how you feel, then I'm going."

"Finally! I've only been telling you to fuck off for about an hour now. Beat it before I slap you again." The stranger descended the steps and turned to look up at me, where I stood elevated on the porch.

"By the way, my name is Skyler." Though not exclusively a boy's name, I was 99% sure that this was a boy. Boys were always sniffing around, trying to find their way into girls' panties. "I'm pleased to meet you, Chelsea."

"We don't need any Good Samaritans, righteous or not, around here," I turned and let myself back in the house, firmly shutting the front door and locking it for good measure.

"Who's here, Chelsea? I hear voices," my mother called out again.

"No one's here," I followed her voice down the hall, cracked open her bedroom door, and stuck my head inside. I was careful to hide my half-naked, disheveled body. "Don't worry, Mom. You're safe."

"I thought I heard someone on the porch," she continued worrying. "Why did you raise your voice?"

"It's nothing," I reassured her.

"You're a wonderful daughter. How could I live without you?"

"The coast is clear. Come out of your room," I smiled, tightlipped from the pain in my knees. "After I get washed up, meet me in the family room, and we'll do the laundry together. Then I'll make dinner."

CHAPTER 2
ADVICE
FRANCINE

Two Hours Later

On the afternoon of the first day of the new school year, I lurked in our cavernous foyer for over an hour, anxiety rising. When I finally heard a step on the front porch, I whipped open the door and beckoned my son to enter.

"Did you miss the bus? I've been worried sick," I scolded as he stepped inside. I couldn't help pausing to admire how the late afternoon sun's rays refracted off the leaded crystal sunburst in the massive oak door. It was the pièce de résistance, our announcement to the gentrifying area that we had arrived.

Skyler still hadn't answered.

"The bus passed two hours ago," I shut the door and turned to face him, thinking what a shame it was that he'd been born a boy. *The older he gets, the more he's a mirror image of me! He'd make a strikingly attractive young woman.* "How did you get home from school?"

"I thought you'd be at work till five. Why are you home this early?"

"The one day I get home early, you're late," I snapped, triggered by a son who seemed to be following in his absentee father's footsteps. "I thought I'd surprise you and cook your favorite stir-fry. That's the last time I try to do something nice for you."

"I didn't miss the bus," said Skyler. "I was helping the neighbor girl. She fell."

"Neighbor girl?" I studied him closely. "Are you talking about the girl in the yellow shack?" Before acquiring the acreage for our custom-built home, I'd inquired around town about the broken-down old farmhouse on a nearby lane. The family that owned it was notorious, and the eyesore presented a drag on property values. I consulted the Zoning Commission and the Health Department, hopeful I'd find a loophole to have the dwelling condemned and torn down.

"I'm not sure what you mean," Skyler said slowly. "There's a girl who lives down the road. Her house may be yellow. I didn't pay attention to details."

"Were you able to assist her?" I sensed a brewing disagreement.

"I picked up her books and papers for her."

"That's the proper Christian attitude," I approved. "But I don't want you to make a habit of associating with *that girl.*"

"*That girl* has a name. It's Chelsea."

"Whatever her name is, I don't want you fraternizing with her."

"Why not?" Skyler's jaw jutted like his father's when refusing to follow my orders.

"If the answer isn't obvious, then, as your mother, I'm a failure."

"What's the obvious answer to you?" he sighed.

"Oh, please! Where do I start?" I crossed my arms. "She may be in your class at school, but she is *not* in our socioeconomic class. Your father is a vice president in his company; I'm an executive, too. That girl's father is a day laborer. If he finds work, it's piecemeal in a factory. They're extremely poor."

"We go to the same school. It doesn't seem very *Christian* not to be friendly with her," Skyler crossed his arms to mirror me. My motherly instinct whispered that now was the moment to nip this teenage friendship in the bud.

"I *was* waiting to make this announcement when we could celebrate with your father, but it's clear that I need to step in to protect you. I've been appointed to the school's Financial Assistance Committee," I paused for Skyler to congratulate me, but all he did was shrug. I continued, "You shouldn't talk to that girl. I know her family's income and background. Her mother receives *disability payments!*"

"You're prejudiced," he accused.

"Not prejudiced," I corrected. "Discerning. There's a big difference. We didn't inherit our wealth, you know. We work hard for what we have. Your father and I want to help you get ahead in life, so we moved here to get you into a prestigious school," although he listened, I sensed that I wasn't making headway. Somehow, I had to get through to him. "I don't want you throwing away your privileged position on some poor white trash. She can't be trusted. Look at her family! She'll try to use you."

Skyler said, "You'll be pleased to know, Mother, that

Chelsea told me to go away. She didn't ask for anything." My suspicions rose higher when he added, "I found her very interesting."

"I don't see what's interesting about someone so far beneath you, Skyler. Did you go to her house?"

"Yes, for a moment."

"You didn't see a mother, did you?"

"Chelsea wouldn't let me inside. She said her mother was sick."

"She's sick, alright! I bet the house was a mess," I predicted.

"It was cluttered and chaotic," he admitted. *Ah,* I thought, *maybe I can rescue my son after all.*

"You're old enough for me to be blunt. That girl's mother is severely mentally ill. She suffers from depression and an acute anxiety disorder. She's afraid to leave the house," I relayed the information I received from Alyssa Jones, another parent. After we met at the upscale supermarket in town and got acquainted over coffee at the new French brasserie, Alyssa had nominated me to join the school's Financial Assistance Committee.

"Try using *that girl's* name," Skyler bristled. "Are you saying you want me to avoid Chelsea because her mother has a mental illness?"

"I'm sorry, son. I know this sounds cold—"

"That's not the proper Christian attitude," he interrupted.

"Let me explain a few things," I put up my hand. "That girl's mother has been mentally ill since she was very young. More than once, she's been hospitalized, forcing the girl to raise herself *and* care for her mother. A mother's mental illness is a burden to a child. It breeds resentment and bad behavior. Plus, mental illness is hereditary."

"How do *you* know all of this shit about her family?"

"I will not tolerate such un-Christian language in this house! Talk like that again, and you'll be grounded," I threatened.

"Ooh, grounded?" Skyler's sarcasm was thick. "As if I care. I never go out, and I don't have any friends. Thanks to *you* for moving us here my senior year!" This outburst was unlike my usually docile son. "I want to know how you know about Chelsea's mother."

"Mrs. Jones, whose daughter is a cheerleader named Kirsten at your school, informed me about the dysfunctional family on our road," I chose my words carefully, hoping he would catch the hint. From what I understood, Kirsten was popular.

"Chelsea could use a friend," Skyler skated past the implied peer pressure. "And a good Christian will always be a friend in need."

"Fine. Be polite to her at school. Smile and wave. That will more than satisfy your Christian duty."

"'Faith without works is dead,'" Skyler dared to preach at me.

I snapped back, "'If someone is caught in a sin, you who live by the Spirit should restore that person gently. But watch yourselves, or you also may be tempted.'"

"Bravo, Mother," Skyler muttered. "You win the duel of the verses today."

"It's not about winning, Skyler. Let someone whose family is more like *that girl's* befriend her," I advised, fighting the familiar fear that I'd raised my son to be soft and weak. "She would wrap an effeminate, emotional boy like you around her finger, and God help us all when that happens!" Silence followed. Perhaps this was the breakthrough moment.

"Let's see if I understand," he finally spoke. "You want to punish an innocent girl for growing up with a sick mother?"

"No, you missed my point. I don't want *you* to get trapped in the web of a family stricken with a mental disorder," I clarified my opposition. "Stay away from that girl. I insist!"

Skyler huffed, turned his back on me without another word, and marched upstairs. He slammed his bedroom door.

CHAPTER 3
WARNING
SKYLER

September

A couple of weeks after Chelsea fell, we again stepped off the bus together. I'd surreptitiously admired her from afar since the first day of school. I liked the way her disheveled strawberry-blonde hair framed her pale, round face. She carried herself defiantly as if nothing from the outside could touch her innermost heart. Trying to catch her sky-blue eyes, I gathered my courage and attempted another conversation.

"Hi, Chelsea," I greeted. "How are your knees healing?"

"Why are you asking?" she politely replied.

"Do you think you'll have scars?"

"Permanent scars will be a reminder of the fall from grace," she intoned as we started walking down the gravel road toward her house.

Confused, I asked, "Meaning?"

"I'm talking about the evil-hearted boys on the bus, of

course!" I wondered if she included me in her condemnation. As if reading my mind, she said, "I'm not sure about you. What are you?" She sounded as curious about me as I was about her. I didn't know how to answer this question; today wasn't the first time it had been asked of me. We walked in silence until Chelsea stopped abruptly.

"Are you going to answer me, or what? If you're going to walk with me, I need to know. Are you a boy or a girl?"

"I'm a boy," I stated emphatically.

"Too bad," she looked disappointed and started walking again. "I secretly hoped you were a girl. I'd prefer a girlfriend."

"Then we have something in common," I joked. "I've searched my entire life for a girlfriend."

"That's not funny. I'm done with boys. I don't trust them. They're all assholes," she eyed me with a gleam I didn't understand. "You look and act like an adorable, mousy little girl. Are you sure you're not a girl?" The teasing touched a nerve.

"For being a victim of the bus boys' treatment, you're sure quick to insult others!"

"Calling you a girl is a compliment, not an insult," she said. "Why are you hanging around me, anyway?"

I shrugged, "No other teenagers in the neighborhood."

"Seeing that the nearest house is a mile down the road, I wouldn't call this a neighborhood."

"You got me," I held up my arms in mock surrender. "You're my only neighbor." We walked in silence. Eventually, Chelsea spoke.

"Never had a neighbor. Don't want a neighbor. You're not required to walk or talk with me," it sounded like I was dismissed.

I ignored her and asked, "How long have you lived here?"

"All my life."

"It's pretty isolated," I commented. "Were you lonely?"

"Watching your house being built, my dad and I were pissed," she growled.

"Why?"

"Do you really want to know?" she stopped and faced me.

"Yes, please."

"Before you built your new house, we *liked* living a mile from the nearest house. We *liked* the open space and living in the country. What we *don't* like is people poking their noses in our family affairs! At least, with your place hidden in the woods, we don't have to look at your freaking ridiculous mansion."

"I wouldn't call our place a mansion," I said defensively.

"Don't bullshit me. You're a spoiled little rich girl. Or boy. Whatever you are, your place is a mansion compared to our dilapidated dump," she paused. Her next words sounded too adult to be coming from a high schooler. "You want to know another reason my dad despises your family? He doesn't want our road gentrified. Next thing you know, you'll want city water, sewers, a paved road, and a bike path. Our taxes will skyrocket, and we'll be forced to move!"

"You have strong opinions," I was impressed with her passion. "By the way, it wasn't *my* decision to move here from the city. It was my parents' decision."

"This is our home," she said earnestly. "We don't want to lose it to a bunch of pretentious one-percenters." Again, I wasn't sure how to respond, but I wanted to know more about this fascinating person.

"So, how did your parents originally choose to move to

this area?" I asked. Chelsea sighed gustily, and we started walking again.

"When my father was twenty-four, he bought forty acres and an abandoned farmhouse. He planned to build a log cabin in the woods. Someday, he hoped to live independently off the land. Mom had a difficult pregnancy with me. After I was born, she got sick. I never knew what was wrong with her, only that she didn't do as much as other moms, and sometimes she was gone for months on end. I learned about her illness when I overheard the school nurse gossiping about her 'breakdown' with the secretary. Dad's dreams of farming to support us were sacrificed to a dark factory because we needed health insurance to care for Mom. Only the land remains from his fantasy, and hopefully, we're not forced to sell it in pieces to rich people like you," she concluded sadly. I couldn't help but feel bad for Chelsea's family and the role families like mine played in their distress.

"How did you start attending private school?" I changed the subject.

"Not my idea. Not my choice," her tone turned brisk. "I messed up at public school." I thought that would be the extent of her answer. To my surprise, she continued. "Well, that's not exactly true. I got expelled from one public school, and I literally got fucked at another," she snuck a sideways glance at me. "Yes, I had sex with a boy at school and got kicked out. Just last February, Dad switched me to this school. That was his behavior modification plan. He promised me the private school environment would be more supportive. Ha! How's that working out, Dad?" she asked the sky.

"I'm sorry. Maybe this year will be better."

"Before you ask, I'll answer," she glossed over my

sympathy. "We can't afford the tuition. But lucky me! I'm a lost cause that became a charity scholarship case. Rich people ease their conscience by giving money to a few dirty outcasts like me."

I said quietly, "Thanks for telling me about your family. You didn't have to tell me about the scholarship."

"I haven't told you anything," she scoffed. We walked silently until we reached the two-track dirt driveway to her house. When we stopped, she faced me and said, "Just because we're neighbors doesn't mean you need to walk with me."

"Some days, I don't want to go home," I admitted.

"Is anyone at your house after school?" She looked interested against her will.

"A couple of days a week, my mother works from home. Today is one of those days."

"My mother's home too," Chelsea smirked. "Let's compare our mothers, shall we? We'll start with yours. Your mom works outside of the house. She's a professional in her right mind. Sane, even," she paused for confirmation.

"Yes," I said. "But that doesn't mean we see eye to eye. We disagree. It's bad since we moved here—" Chelsea held up her hand.

"Let me finish. My mother doesn't work. She's not a professional. She's fucking insane. She has a disease, a mental illness. That's what all the doctors tell Dad and me anyway. She's nothing like your mother or anyone else's. Got it?" I nodded mutely as she stared me down. "You're lucky you can argue with your mother. You may disagree, but I dare say she's rational. Go home, rich kid," she dismissed me again. "Go talk to your mother. I bet she even bakes homemade cookies for you!"

"Baking cookies is not my mom's style," I deflected.

Hoping she wouldn't slap me for what I was about to say, I took a deep breath. "Do you want some company? I could walk you the rest of the way."

"You're obviously not listening, idiot. *My mother has a mental illness,*" she hissed. "That's why no one comes over!"

"Growing up, didn't you ever have a play date with a friend at your house?" I couldn't wrap my mind around this girl's solitary upbringing.

"I didn't have time for a friend. I had to get home to check on Mom. Clean, do laundry, cook, and wash dishes. Things most mothers do to care for their children," she radiated fury. "If I even had a friend today, I couldn't invite them over. The place is a freaking pigpen. You saw it!"

I nodded reluctantly and gathered my courage to say, "I'd like to meet your mother."

"Maybe I need to use some language you can comprehend," Chelsea shook her head exasperatedly. "My mother is wack. She's cray-cray—nuts, bonkers, out of her mind. You couldn't handle meeting her, and she could not deal with meeting you. End of story."

"I guess I'll see you tomorrow on the bus," I didn't want to say goodbye, but she was clearly not about to change her mind.

"Not if I can help it," she turned on her heel.

"Bye, Chelsea," I called after her retreating back. She didn't turn around but did lift her right hand in a backward salute.

I walked home, where my mother ambushed me again at the door.

"The bus passed an hour ago! Where were you?"

"Talking with someone at the bus stop."

"Oh, no, you don't, young man," she threatened as I

moved past her to climb the stairs to my room. "Get back here! Someone at the bus stop was that neighbor girl, right?"

"Yes. I talked with Chelsea for a few minutes."

"You mean sixty minutes," Mom corrected.

"So, what?"

"Don't backtalk me, mister," she snapped. "You disobeyed a direct order! I told you to avoid that low-class girl."

"What is your problem, Mother?"

"Don't be ignorant, Skyler. She's a scholarship student, and her mother is mentally ill," she crossed her arms. "She and her crude parents will not be around long anyway. I plan to weed them out of the neighborhood."

Disgusted by her snobbishness, I said, "We're the inter-lopers, Mother, can't you see that? *We* moved into *their* tranquil paradise! They think we're rude for building out here."

"That's absurd," she laughed a high, fake laugh. "We have every right to build here. They're just jealous of our money. Which is another good reason for not getting involved with that girl and her ungrateful welfare family."

"Talking with *Chelsea* for a few minutes after school is not getting involved with her or her family," I intentionally emphasized the name my mother seemed to detest.

"You don't need to get huffy, Skyler. I'm giving you good motherly advice. That charity case is too—" she eyed me as if to gauge how far she could go with her criticism. "How should I say it? She's too hefty for you," Mom blurted. My mouth fell open.

"That's awful," I said when I recovered from the shock.

"Before you criticize me, listen," she reached out to place her hand on my forearm, but I recoiled. "I saw her after meeting the dean at school. There's no nice way of saying it. She's obese. I can tell she's always struggled with her weight."

"Her weight's not your business," this was a minefield I recognized. My mother monitored everything she ate. Food was her obsession, or rather, starving from lack of food. She didn't diet; she followed a militant menu plan. On the rare occasion we indulged in dessert, she served us each one minuscule scoop of ice cream in a kiddie cone.

"One of the seven deadly sins is gluttony," quipped Mom with a pious glance heavenward. "If you get involved with her, she'll carry her weight into a relationship. Her weight will become your business and my business."

"You're getting ahead of yourself," I warned. "I think Chelsea looks nice. She's attractive."

"If she lost thirty pounds, she might be attractive. Sadly that's unlikely to happen."

"Mother, what would the pastor think? The bible says judge not, lest ye be judged!"

"I'm not judging; I'm being honest. Plain and simple, Chelsea is fat."

"She's voluptuous," I countered with a word that had caught my attention in the book we were reading for senior literature class.

"*Voluptuous?*" Mom looked scandalized. "Don't you dare use that word in my house, young man! It's the equivalent of using the word whore or prostitute."

"Voluptuous is a literary term for a well-proportioned attractive woman," I corrected her. "During the romantic art period, voluptuous women were considered the most beautiful."

"Stop," she covered her ears like a toddler. "That word is vulgar in the twenty-first century! It's pornographic."

"Really, Mom, pornographic?" I knew from the look on

her face that she was likely to explode, but I couldn't stop myself. "What do you even know about porn?"

"You're being foulmouthed and disrespectful," she pointed at me forcefully. "Stop arguing this instant!"

"I like curvy girls," I said.

"Curvy girls? What do you know about curvy? 'Curvy woman' is a code word for a slut!"

"Whatever you say. Mother knows best," sarcasm dripped from my voice.

"If you think a female is sexy, stay away from her, Skyler. Sexy is not a desirable quality. Not at this age or any age," she lectured. "As for your big friend, she has a big problem. Someone needs to intervene before her obesity destroys her."

I itched to shut her up, so I said, "I read in *Cosmo* that some women like their curves. They like having flesh on their bones." With a foreboding glance, she took up a new argument.

"Obesity is an employability issue. I wouldn't have my marketing job if I were fat like your friend. To my clients, I *am* the company. I need to look good to attract new clients. Fat does not look good and does not project a successful, positive, healthy image," she paused. When I didn't respond, she pressed harder. "Your classmate is grossly over-weight. If she can't learn to exercise self-control, she'll limit her opportunities in life. Everyone knows obesity is not only a health problem. It's an emotional and behavioral problem."

"Not everyone wants to be thin like you, Mother. You're damn near anorexic," I turned my back on her and stalked away.

"Get back here, young man. I'm not finished talking to you!" I climbed the stairs, entered my bedroom, and slammed the door. She shouted from the bottom of the stair-case, "When your father comes home, I'll tell him every-thing you said. You'll be in huge trouble!" I knew these were idle threats. Dad rarely came home anymore; he traveled three out of four weeks, most months. I was starting to understand why he wanted to be gone on business trips so often.

I lay down on my bed and gazed at the ceiling. I thought about Chelsea. Mom had been spot-on about one of her observations. To me, Chelsea was sexy. I imagined her beautiful, bright face. I remembered her great-looking legs from where I'd crouched, staring at them when she was bleeding after her 'fall from grace.' I laughed inwardly, recalling her description of the accident at the bus stop.

More important than her physique, I liked Chelsea's spunk. She was a survivor, and I admired that. She was my worldly, strong, independent, mature, forbidden friend.

CHAPTER 4
SECRETS
CHELSEA

October

As the bus neared my stop, I gathered my things. A boy in the seat behind me cracked a fat joke. I ignored it. The barrage from the boys sitting further back, however, I couldn't ignore.

"Chelsea's on welfare," one of them hissed. "Free lunch freeloader."

"Trailer trash," spouted another.

"Not just trash! A whore," the one who cracked the first joke took back the mic. "She's a dirty fucking whore. I know three guys from Central High that screwed her. She got off on being gang-banged." I dropped my backpack and stepped to the edge of his bench. Fear and defiance shone in his eyes. Standing firm, I punched him with a right hook directly in his temple. His head rocked sideways. He slumped in his seat. I turned, picked up my backpack, and walked off the bus.

As I alighted on the dirt road with my heart pounding, I wondered, *Did I knock the prick temporarily unconscious? Or permanently?* It happened so fast; the driver never saw a thing. When the bus pulled away, I caught Skyler watching me intently. Although he'd occasionally walked me home after school for the past month, I still clung to my view of boys as despicable. I was unsure if he was an exception; something made me want to trust him.

"I can walk by myself, you know," I said as we started down the gravel lane. "You don't need to accompany me home every day."

"I don't. Three days a week, I walk with you. The other two days, my mother expects me to go directly home."

"Are there chores she expects you to do?"

"No. She doesn't want me to spend time with you."

"That's refreshing," I snapped. "At least you're being honest. Your mother never met me. What's her problem?"

Skyler answered matter-of-factly, "She's controlling and wants me to go out with rich girls. Daughters of her friends."

"So, you're slumming it with me?"

"Nope."

"Then you're rebelling? Using me to piss off your mother?"

"None of the above. I like you," he replied cheerfully.

"You must be lying. Or are you delusional?"

"If you won't take a compliment, that's your choice," he laughed. I allowed myself to smile at him. Maybe he wasn't so bad. Mom was inside as usual when we arrived at my house. Her mental state worsened after Skyler's unintentional visit on the first day of school. Months had passed since she set foot outdoors. I knew she needed to return to long-term treatment, but our insurance had already covered all the time allowed for the year.

Skyler looked surprised when I said, "Wait for me at the front gate." I went in to tell Mom I was going for a walk with the new neighbor boy.

"Don't invite him in," she looked frightened. "I'm not presentable."

"We'll stay outside," I promised. "We'll go around the house. When we pass the kitchen, you can peek at us through the blinds if you want. You'll see, he's kind of cute." Mom looked surprised. Before she could ask any questions, I outlined the rest of our itinerary. "We're going to walk through the field, then down the path into the woodlot."

"Be careful to keep your wits about you," she pulled her bathrobe tightly around her waist. "Don't let him take advantage."

"Don't worry, Mom. Skyler's a nice boy. Besides, I can defend myself," I kissed the top of her head, said goodbye, and stepped outside.

"Skyler, I want to show you something," he jumped a little when I took his hand in mine. We began walking. "If you promise never to tell anyone, I'll take you to one of my favorite hiding places."

"Where is it?" he looked cautiously curious.

"Just trust me." I decided to tease him a little. "You already turned eighteen, right," it was more a statement than a question. He stopped in his tracks.

"Yes, why do you ask?"

"An older girl can't take any chances," I chortled.

"How much older?" he looked positively petrified now.

"I missed some school, you know. Got held back. I turn nineteen next month." He seemed to relax a little. I steered him around the house and past the kitchen as I promised

Mom I would. Although we only owned forty acres, our property was adjacent to a state forest and a private wildlife conservation area. It was beautiful, peaceful, and quiet. Skyler seemed out of his element in this unmanicured setting. I guided him deep into a grove of towering trees.

"Isn't it lovely?" I stopped under the giant canopy of the biggest tree and breathed the pungent piney perfume.

"Breathtaking."

"Me or the woods?" I asked boldly. His face flushed, and he looked away without answering. "I'm just having fun with you," I relished the discomfort he tried to cover up. "Let's sit."

"On pine needles?"

"Yes, of course. One pine needle is prickly. A bed of pine needles is soft. Come on, let's sit," I repeated. Skyler still hesitated. I stood before him and placed my hands on his shoulders. "Don't be shy. I won't bite," I pushed firmly down, and he folded like a camping chair. Once seated, his leg started bouncing nervously. He wouldn't look up at me. My wool skirt flared outward when I squatted to sit across from him. *Shit,* I thought, *did I flash him?* I tugged the skirt mid-thigh, covering myself. My bare knee brushed against his. His eyes grew round, and he took a deep breath. I recognized these tell-tale signs! He'd never sat this close to a girl. Despite his nerves, or maybe because of them, he started talking.

"It's so quiet. No road noises. No manmade sounds at all. I can even hear the breeze in the pines."

"Glad you like my refuge from the world," I smiled.

"Is this where you take all your boyfriends?" the question sounded slightly accusatory.

Looking into his soulful dark brown eyes, I teased more aggressively, "This is where I hike up my skirt, sit on top of you, and fuck your brains out." Skyler flinched. For a second, I thought he would run. "Silly boy! I'm not serious. I don't have boyfriends. Never have," I laughed and smacked his leg companionably. "If I did have one, I wouldn't bring him here. You're the only person I've brought to my sanctuary. You're not like other boys."

"Is that good, bad, or weird?"

"I'm paying you a compliment," I explained. "For a boy, you're kind. Sensitive."

"All my life, when I've been told 'you're not like other boys,' it was said with contempt. People teased me for being androgynous," he looked down at his body. "I've been called awful names and beaten up more than once for looking like a girl." I'd never met a boy willing to talk about his feelings.

"Exhibiting feminine qualities or acting like a girl is not bad."

"Gender is so complicated," he sighed. "For a girl, you're exceptionally tough. But I saw you smack the short-haired punk on the bus over something he said. What was it?"

"Called me a whore," I growled.

"That's terrible. Why are they so vicious? Why would he call you a, uh, a...," he couldn't repeat the slur I used so casually.

"Be straight with me. Say the word," I ordered.

It took a few seconds, but he managed to eke out, "Whore." It looked like he might vomit. "Right. Nasty. Never a good word," he added meekly.

"Say it louder."

"I don't reference women in those terms," he pushed back.

"We're alone in the woods. No one is going to hear you,

Skyler! Repeat after me: 'Chelsea, you're a cheap fucking whore.'"

"No."

"Be real with me," I challenged. "Live in my world."

He sat silent and still for a moment, then said forcefully, "Fucking whore!" The vomitous look was back. "There, are you satisfied?"

"Yes," I nodded slowly. "Strong women threaten men. Boys are afraid of me. They're always trying to keep me in my place. Always afraid I might talk—" I stopped mid-sentence.

"Talk about what?" Skyler asked after a beat. I wasn't sure if I could trust him with more truth. Sure, he was different. Not like other boys. *However, that doesn't mean anything,* I reminded myself with a wry smile. *I don't trust girls, either.* My first rule of survival was, don't get close to anyone. I searched Skyler's lovely brown eyes. I decided to test him.

"Promise not to tell anyone?" Mentally, I crossed my fingers. *If he keeps his mouth shut, I have a friend.* Before I graduated from high school, I wanted one friend. Just one! I grabbed one of his idle hands and held it.

"I promise," he pledged. "Your secret is safe with me."

I took a deep breath and began, "I used to crave acceptance from my classmates. I wanted so badly to be part of the in-crowd. That was my first mistake," I wasn't sure how to proceed. I twirled a pine needle between the fingers of the hand Skyler wasn't holding.

"Everyone makes mistakes," he encouraged.

"Last year, at my other school, I got invited to some kid's house party in town. I was so excited to be included. When my date and I arrived, it was overwhelming. There was dancing and drinking and people making out in every corner. I chugged a few beers. Took a few shots of hard stuff from a bottle being passed around," I looked at Skyler's face to gauge his reaction. He seemed unbothered so far. "I drank way too much and got totally shit-faced. That was my second mistake."

"Drinking is risky business," he noted.

"I started to feel dizzy while we were dancing, and I nearly barfed on the living room carpet. My date took me to an upstairs bathroom. After puking my guts out, he guided me into a bedroom. Letting him do that was my third mistake," I paused again, weighing my words while Skyler waited. "I passed out on the bed. Eventually, I came to in a haze. My so-called date was heavy on top of me. He was a big muscular guy; I couldn't move. I couldn't stop him. Each time he thrust himself inside me, he muttered, 'dumb cunt.'"

"I'm so sorry," Skyler whispered. "I've never been to a house party, but I heard shit like that can happen," he squeezed my hand lightly.

"There's more," I warned. "As I lay there, I recalled I'd been wearing a red tank top. It and all my other clothing were nowhere to be seen. I began to wonder, did I willingly strip for him? Maybe in my drunken stupor, I said yes. Maybe I begged for it. I don't remember. Honestly, I was a hot mess. It wasn't the first time I got drunk and had sex," I wanted Skyler to know the whole truth.

"Consent or no consent, if you're intoxicated, no one should take advantage of you!"

"It's worse than a question of consent," I said, emotion rising. "Did the monster leave the room after he got his rocks off? No! He grabbed my ponytail and jerked my head backward. I thought he snapped my neck. Then, his fingers pressed down on my throat. I couldn't speak. I couldn't scream." Skyler's eyes got big. I watched his pupils dilate from fear. I didn't let it stop me. "It was dark, but I sensed someone watching in the room. The scumbags! I was scared out of my mind. I thought I was going to die. When I was about to pass out, the voyeur said, 'Hey, man. That's enough,' and my date let go," I stared into Skyler's eyes. "Is it totally sick that I was thankful he was there?"

"I don't know," he barely breathed.

"Neither do I," I shrugged. "As they were leaving, one of them said, 'The fat bitch is a lousy fuck.' They laughed at me. The laughter hurt. I remember the laughter," I invested my darkest secret in Skyler, trusting he wouldn't trade on it to hurt me in the future. Although I didn't want to cry, huge drops rolled down my cheeks.

"That's terrible, Chelsea. You were brutally assaulted," Skyler touched my face and wiped away my tears. It sounded like he might cry, too. "Why do you remember the laughter?"

"I can't forget it! I was humiliated. Degraded. Subhuman. They discarded me like a worthless piece of trash. You know, though the physical pain didn't last long, when a boy laughs at me today, the laughter of my rapists is rekindled deep inside me."

"What'd you do afterward?"

"I found my clothes and purse, scrambled downstairs, and out the front door. I don't remember the people or the party scene. I remember the cold night air," my eyes were unfocused as I recalled the gruesome details. "I have flashbacks of standing on the dark porch of an empty hardware store. Everything was pitch black except for a lamp on a distant corner. I remember standing there, bare ass naked to the world, pulling on my skirt."

"That must have been so scary for you," Skyler wrapped his hands tightly around mine.

"It's the strangest thing. I was frantic because I lost my panties," a brittle laugh escaped me, shattering the silent glade around us. "I remember wishing I could go find them and put them on to stop the semen from dripping down my leg. I was embarrassed and terrified the pricks would chase me. Hunt for me. Maybe strangle me to death. Their words spun around in my head. Haunted me. Standing alone, outside, without a friend in the world, I believed I *was* a dumb cunt."

"That's awful," Skyler shuddered. "How did you escape?"

"Fortunately, my phone was still in my purse. I called my dad at work. I waited for him to pick me up. By the time he arrived, the chilly night air had sobered me up."

"I don't know what to say," Skyler said tenderly. "I'm sad for you."

"Don't be," I shook my head. "My dad was relieved to see me. He didn't press for details. He promised to listen if I needed to talk. He told me over and over that he loved me. I cried, not because I got raped, but for disappointing my father. He'd warned me not to attend a drinking party."

"Your dad sounds like a good man."

"He is," I nodded. "He didn't judge me. He loved and accepted me. Halfway home, we pulled into a vacant parking lot. Daddy held me until I stopped crying."

"I can't even imagine how horrible that night was," empathized Skyler.

"Worst night of my life," I agreed. "At the same time, it was enlightening. I learned that I am loved. I have a loving father."

"Yes, you do," Skyler exclaimed. "Your father's love reflects the unconditional love of our heavenly Father, God." Startled by the mention of religion, I checked

Skyler's face to see if he was mocking me. Nothing but innocent admiration was reflected there.

"If God exists, he lives in my father's heart. Ironically, that night, I vowed I would never love another man besides my father. I would never crave attention or inclusion again. I would never trust anyone again. I would never allow anyone to hurt me again."

"What happened the next day?"

"Before sunrise, I took myself to the downtown women's clinic and got the morning-after pill. I looked like hell. My thighs were raw, and my throat was turning purple and blue. A nurse wanted to examine me and started talking about a rape kit. She threatened to call the police or a social worker at the women's shelter. I lied. Told her I was hungover and that I liked rough sex," I laughed nervously.

"Did you ever talk to anyone about it?"

"Hell, no! Only you. Don't you dare tell anyone. You promised," I glared at him.

"I won't say a word," Skyler repeated his promise. We sat quietly, each lost in private thought. Pretty soon, I started to regret my transparency. *I can't believe I told him about being humiliated,* I worried. *Fucking great way to start a friendship, Chelsea!* But as quickly as the doubts arose, they dissipated. I knew I didn't want his friendship if Skyler couldn't handle my darkest hour.

"Over the summer, one of my assailants talked to kids from our supposed *Christian* school," I offered a postscript. "He told the jerks I enjoyed getting gang banged. That's why the boy on the bus called me a whore. I'll ignore white trash, fat jokes, and even jokes about Mom, but I won't tolerate their lies about being abused."

"Will you ever go to the police?"

"Are you nuts? If I go to the cops, I'll be expelled and arrested."

"You?" he was bewildered.

"Yes, me. I have a record. Fortunately, what crimes I committed were misdemeanors. And I was a minor."

"Sorry. That's tough," he sounded different than when he was comforting me over the rape.

"My family was broke, Skyler," I felt compelled to defend my actions. "Down to our last dollar and over-whelmed with debt. We were too proud to go to the food bank, so we missed a few meals. I was starving but couldn't go against my parents' wishes. The first time, I got caught stealing junk food. Chips, crackers, cookies, candy bars. The second time, I got caught shoplifting tampons. I told the judge I wasn't sorry. 'Lock me up,' I said, 'I'll be damned if I'm going without tampons!'"

"I'm sorry you went through that," he had the good grace to blush a little. "You really should report what happened, Chelsea. You're the victim of a felony."

"I'm no victim, and I'll prove it," I scoffed. "I can defend myself. Didn't you see me? I slugged that loser so hard today that I may be arrested for attempted murder. If one more cocksucker calls me a whore or a slut, I'll kill them," I declared with finality. Skyler looked a little scared. "There's a bright side," I tried to lighten the mood. "If I get arrested, the assholes won't have Chelsea to kick around anymore."

"I can help you file a report," he offered.

"Against whom, exactly?"

"You know the name of your date, right?"

"Yes, and I also know what he'll say," I sighed at Skyler's naiveté. "He'll say I wanted to have sex with two boys."

"Then file a report against the parents of the boy hosting the party," exhorted my would-be savior.

"Come on, Skyler. This isn't some TV crime drama," I shook my head. "I'm not reporting anything because *no one will believe me.*"

"But it's not your fault!" Skyler was fully embodying his Good Samaritan. It was time to share the rest of my history to knock some sense into him.

"There's more backstory. I was in eighth grade when I started having sex with boys. By ninth grade, I'd learned to seduce them."

"Why?" he looked stunned.

"My counselor said I was desperate to be loved. I say, try going through elementary and middle school without one friend! Besides name-calling, not one classmate spoke to me throughout all those years. So, I looked for any way to get attention. Boys couldn't resist flirtation, even from someone like me. Like a drug, I got a short-lived rush from sex. I've slept with more guys in town than I can count. I don't want to know their names. I don't care. The night I attended the fateful party, I already had a reputation for being an easy lay," I paused to scrutinize his face. "You see? No one will believe me."

"I believe you," he said gently.

"Oh, Skyler, you're so innocent," I laughed a little too sharply in his face. He recoiled but didn't relinquish his hold on my hand. Quickly, I got to my knees, leaned forward, and kissed him on his forehead. I lingered a moment, then licked his eyelid and kissed him on the lips. He responded. As I stuck my tongue in his mouth, I pushed him back on the bed of pine needles and straddled his torso. After a few minutes of passionate kissing, I pulled back, caught my breath, and stood up. Lying prone beneath me, Skyler stared up my skirt, brown eyes huge. I guessed his thoughts.

"We're not having sex," I reached down to help him up. I held him in a long, tight hug before we brushed the needles from our clothes. We walked out of the white pine forest holding hands. On the way back to my house, we didn't speak. Every other minute, I turned my head to look at Skyler. I smiled. He smiled back. We laughed playfully.

For the first time, I'd found a friend.

CHAPTER 5
RECKONING
SKYLER

Two Hours Later

Walking to my house at dusk after leaving Chelsea by her front gate, I watched a thick fog settle across the fields. The autumn evening air was heavy, cool, and sweet. I floated through the mist. I fell in love with the girl next door.

At home, my mother greeted me with another tirade.

"Where have you been, young man? I called the school. They said you got on the bus. I was worried sick!"

"Sorry, I was next door with Chelsea. I lost track of time." Mom's eyes narrowed, and the interrogation began.

"What were you doing with her?"

"We went for a walk."

"Where?"

"Nowhere," I shrugged. "Just around."

"Around where?"

"Down the road and around her property. Why are you shouting at me?" I raised my voice to match hers.

"I told you to stay away from that girl," she continued to yell. "She has a bad reputation and will get you in trouble!"

"What do *you* know about her reputation?" It was meant to be rhetorical.

"All of the decent parents know which kids have bad reputations. I've heard about Chelsea. That girl is loose, a hussy. Watch yourself, or she'll entrap you. Mark my words, Skyler."

"You shouldn't believe gossip," I dismissed her motherly hysteria. "It's not a very Christian thing to do."

"This is a small community. People know each other's business."

"The boys at school spread lies about her. She's done nothing wrong," I defended my new friend.

"You don't understand the risks," she renewed some of the same objections she'd tried to impress upon me on the first day of school. "Compared to her family, we're rich. She'll try to get her claws into you to get our money. I hate to be so blunt, but she may entice you, maybe even try to have sex with you! Then, she'll pretend she's pregnant to get more money out of us," Mom predicted. "If she gets pregnant, we'll be paying child support for eighteen wretched years."

"Chelsea would never exploit me or anyone else," it was taking some effort to keep a lid on my rage.

"Skyler, she's street smart. You're too naïve to see it. For years, she's been forced to fend for herself! Did you forget that her mother is mentally ill? *That girl* is predisposed to the same defects. Does your reputation mean nothing to you?"

Shaking my head in disbelief, I refused to indulge her in

her tantrum. I turned my back on my mother, climbed the stairs, and sat at my desk in my bedroom. I couldn't believe she didn't shout after me or chase me upstairs to continue haranguing.

A few minutes later, I heard her speaking. Curiosity ablaze, I crept halfway down the stairs to eavesdrop. While I only heard Mom's side of the conversation, I could imagine the voice on the other end of the line. She was talking with her new best friend, Mrs. Jones.

"Yes, thank you for the reminder, Alyssa! I plan to be at the meeting. I'm already working on the fundraising plans with the Foundation's treasurer," she affirmed in the politest, calmest voice imaginable. I wondered at the massive shift in her energy following our disagreement only a few moments earlier.

My ears perked up when she said, "A dinner invitation? Why, thank you! I'd love nothing more." I stifled a groan, knowing what would come next. "Regrettably, my husband can't join us. He won't be home. He travels extensively for work. But Skyler will be happy to accompany me. Will your daughter be there, as well? I've heard what a delightful young lady she is from some of the other parents," she buttered up her friend. A moment of silence passed.

"Thanks for asking. I'm sorry to say that Skyler is struggling to adjust. Unfortunately, he's not outgoing like his mother," she chortled. "He still hasn't made any friends." A short pause. "Yes, that's true. It's early in the term." This time, she listened for a long time before answering Mrs. Jones more guardedly.

"I wouldn't say he *hangs out* with Chelsea. He's merely polite to her at school," I rolled my eyes at my mother's deliberate mischaracterization of my new acquaintance. "Thank you, Alyssa. You're too kind. I did my best to raise him to be considerate of others. Sometimes, he doesn't know when enough is enough." The next turn in the one-sided conversation reignited my anger with my two-faced mother.

"Shoplifting?" she sounded scandalized. "Kicked out of public school – no! Why did that happen?" I held my breath, waiting for things to get worse. "Thanks for letting me know. I'll be sure Skyler keeps his distance from *that girl* in the future," she bought whatever gossip Mrs. Jones sold her hook, line, and sinker. "If you hear more about Chelsea, please let me know." A minute passed.

"Oh, coffee after the meeting? Sure. Anything special on your mind?" I could tell her interest was piqued. "Really? The school board? I'm flattered," now she sounded enthusiastic. "Okay, it's a date. Coffee's on me," she offered magnanimously. "So true! The real business always takes place after the formal meeting," she agreed before bidding her friend adieu.

I crept back upstairs, reflecting on the overheard conversation and my experience starting my senior year in a new school against my will. If my mother knew the truth, she'd be humiliated. Making new friends was too daunting a prospect. I recalled standing in the crowded cafeteria during lunch hour earlier in the day. Everyone was gathered in their well-established friendship groups. *I don't belong here,* I thought. I didn't dare approach a table full of unfamiliar faces. Since no one invited me to join them, I sat alone at a table in the corner.

While I ate, I noticed Chelsea pay the cashier and enter the cafeteria with her lunch tray. One of the popular kids whistled loudly as she walked past their table. Chelsea tilted her head a little higher and promenaded around the cafeteria, looking for a place to sit. On her second lap, she noticed me. We made eye contact, and I nodded in recognition.

She approached and asked, "May I sit with you?"

"Sure," I said.

"Don't be so sure. Look around. Everyone's watching us. If you let me sit at this table, you're doomed. Your chances of hanging out with the rich, goody-goody church-going students will plummet. Guaranteed."

"Please join me," I ignored her doomsaying. "I prefer your company to the supermodels across the room," I winced at my choice of words. "That didn't sound right. Sorry. I get nervous around girls like you."

"Don't try to flatter me, and never say I didn't warn you. Your social life in this school is finished. To those kids, I'm an abomination. The personification of evil."

"No, you're not. You're my rescuer. I don't want to sit alone. Everyone will think I'm a geek," I joked. She was still standing, so I waved at the empty table. "Go ahead, take your pick."

"You're worse than a geek," laughed Chelsea. "You're either a nerdy nuisance, or you're the most courageous and independent freethinker I've ever met," she settled into the seat across from me, and I admired her eyes. They were bright, clear, and blue. I thought about how pretty she looked, then bowed my head.

"What're you doing?" Chelsea asked rudely.

"Praying," I looked up at her.

"Why?"

"Giving thanks."

"For what, exactly?"

"You can join me or listen," I bowed my head again and spoke quietly. "Dear God, thank you for my many blessings: this food, every breath I take, a beautiful day, and a new friend. I am thankful Chelsea is willing to sit with me. Amen." Chelsea was staring at me when I looked up.

"To the kids across the cafeteria, you don't exist, you know," she said bitterly. "If they believe in God and they're disgusting assholes, how can you believe in their God?"

"That's a deep question," I was excited that she took an interest in what I had to say. "Maybe they're misguided. Or possibly they're not the problem. Perhaps I offended them, or I don't understand them. We're taught that we live in a world seeking to separate us from the love of God and others. Why should I allow my perception of others to undermine my relationship with God?" I tried to answer the dilemma she outlined.

"You're so strange," wonderment replaced the bitterness in her voice. As we began to eat, our conversation shifted to the classes we liked and disliked. Chelsea soon asked, "They're still watching us, aren't they?"

"Yes, the boys from our bus keep turning around to look at us."

"Should we give them something to talk about? Wanna play footsie?" I wasn't sure how to take this bold challenge. I wasn't even sure she liked me much until she asked me to sit with me! She licked her lips ostentatiously.

"You wouldn't dare," my heart started to pound. Under the table, she kicked off her shoe and pressed her foot between my legs.

"Try me. Bet I could give you an orgasm in one minute."

"Um, uh," I stammered, completely taken off guard. "We're in the cafeteria," was all I could say.

"Just leaning into my reputation," she threw back her head and laughed too loud. The bell rang. "Saved by the bell," she quipped, slowly removing her foot from my crotch.

In a rush of courage, I said, "Lunch tomorrow. Sit with me?"

Chelsea studied my face earnestly, then said, "Skyler, you're such a loser. If you insist, it's a date." We got up and walked out of the cafeteria together. Everyone watched us.

While I hadn't understood at the time, at least following our talk on the bed of pine needles, I understood better why she'd said such things. It was still unclear whether she wanted to be friends or have sex with me. Or maybe she was using me. I mused on the situation until, at six o'clock, Mom called me for dinner.

Downstairs, I served myself from the pots on the stove and carried my plate into the family room to watch the evening news. I didn't say a word to my mother the whole meal. After I finished, I cleared my plate and retreated to my bedroom. Although I tried, I couldn't unearth the motivation to study. Shortly before ten, I washed up, climbed into bed, and switched on my reading lamp. As I struggled to read a novel, there was a knock on my bedroom door. I heard my mother's voice.

"Skyler, are you still awake? May I come in?" Without waiting for permission, Mom entered my room and sat on the edge of my bed. "Son, I'm sorry we had harsh words earlier today. During our first year of marriage, your father always insisted that we did not end the day on a sore note."

"Mom, it's late, and I'm exhausted. What do you have to say?"

"Now, I don't want you to get upset," my shoulders slumped at this beginning. "When I discourage you from seeing *that girl*, it's only because I have your best interests at heart. I love you, and I want you to be successful."

"Chelsea, Chelsea, Chelsea," I said sharply. "Must we talk about her again?"

"Please hear me out and consider my point of view. Today, I spoke with Mrs. Jones. She's Kirsten's mom, you know, Kirsten from your school?" I looked blankly at her, waiting for her to go on. She finally did. "Without my asking, Alyssa illuminated Chelsea's troubled past."

"Mom, I don't want to hear more gossip about my friend. It's not like we're dating; she's *my friend*."

"I'm not gossiping, and I resent the implication. According to Alyssa, you were with Chelsea at school today. You had lunch with her at a table for two!" I sighed at the absurdly twisted truth. "People are starting to talk, Skyler. Do you really want to be associated with a promiscuous teenage girl? Aren't you interested in protecting your reputation?"

"No, Mother, I have little interest in my so-called reputation that you're so worried about. I don't care what the popular kids think about me."

She drew her eyebrows together and asked earnestly, "Why not, son?"

"The popular kids expect everyone to conform. If I wanted to hang out with them and be accepted, I'd have to hide my true self. I'm not interested in making friends that don't like me for who I am," I said. She pressed her lips together and seemed to contemplate my answer.

"If you don't care about your reputation, then, at least, you should care about mine. You're embarrassing me," admitted my mother. "Mrs. Jones and the superintendent plan to nominate me to serve on the school board. Eventually, my service on the board will help me get elected to the county commission," she revealed the full extent of her ambition.

"Finally, you're being honest with me," I burst out. "You

admit you care more about your reputation than my feelings!"

"Everyone appreciates my businesslike, no-nonsense approach," Mom ignored me. "Let me tell you the cornerstone of my school board campaign platform. If a family with a student at one of our schools receives financial aid, they must volunteer several hours weekly at the school or in the community. How does that sound?"

"Sounds misguided," I shot her down. "Don't most students who receive financial assistance only have one parent? A single parent would have to work a lot to support their family, maybe even have two jobs. Why would you pile on another burden?" Mom looked astonished.

"The Bible reads, 'the poor of this world we will always have with us.' They need to start earning their way. That's what being a good Christian leader is all about—showing them the way, guiding them, and reinforcing the Lord's will when necessary. You're ignorant and foolish," she sniped.

Stung, I said, "Sorry that I'm your greatest disappointment in life, Mother. I wish you could accept me as I am and be happy for me. I accept *you* even when I disagree with you. And I'm happy for you finding your purpose now that you uprooted our family and moved us here."

"Let's talk more tomorrow," she glossed over what I said. "Tonight, let's end on a hopeful, positive note. My new friend, Alyssa, invited us to dinner at their house."

"You and Dad can go have a good time."

"You know your dad won't go. He's traveling. You're coming with me. I understand Kirsten is a lovely girl," she put on her solicitous voice.

"Awkward," I said in falsetto.

"Don't blow this opportunity to be part of the in-group! Kirsten is a popular cheerleader at your school, Skyler. She has *influence*. All the kids are aware you befriended that despicable Chelsea. *They* know better than to associate with a lowlife troublemaker. Why don't you?"

"Mother, I'm warning you. Don't press me about Chelsea."

"At least expand your circle of friends, Skyler," she switched to an encouraging tone. "Think about Alyssa's daughter. She may be sweet. She may be your type."

"Sorry to disappoint you again, Mom," I wouldn't be swayed. "I don't have a type. Never had a girlfriend."

"Why not consider Kirsten for that role? I saw her at your school. She's cute, and Alyssa told me dozens of boys are interested in her." Kirsten did not sound like someone I would like, but I was tired of this endless debate with my mother.

"Fine," I said. "I'll look for Kirsten at school."

"There, wasn't that easy?" Mom clapped with glee. "I'm so happy we're making progress. Remember, if you date a girl, you're dating her family and their good name."

"Mom, did you appreciate Alyssa's dinner invitation?"

"Yes, indeed. Alyssa is demonstrating a genuine gift of Christian hospitality to welcome us to the community," she piped piously, as I expected.

"If you believe in Christian hospitality, we should invite Chelsea and her parents for dinner."

"Don't be ridiculous, Skyler. It's not the same thing at all," she looked appalled. "I told you; they're not our kind of people. Chelsea's family is emblematic of the school's mission. And you must always remember, never marry the mission." When I didn't respond, she reverted to begging, "Skyler, I'm pleading with you! Ask Kirsten on a date. Stop humiliating me. Be done with Chelsea. No more Chelsea!"

I turned on my side, facing away from her, and said,

"Good night, Mother. Please turn off the light on your way out." I felt her slight weight lift off the mattress's edge. The light clicked off a second later.

"You're going to ruin my reputation and all my chances for happiness in our new home, Skyler. I hope you're happy," she shut my door.

CHAPTER 6
INNOCENT
CHELSEA

November

Every day following our walk in the woods, Skyler and I sat together at lunch. It became a standing date that I unexpectedly enjoyed. I came to know him as odd, quiet, and reticent. Despite being a boy, he never gave me cause to doubt or mistrust him in this public setting. Likewise, every day when the bus departed our dusty drop-off point after school, Skyler approached me. Today, he seemed unusually awkward, confused, and undecided.

"What's your deal?" I asked.

"Nothing," he blushed.

"Something's obviously on your mind. Either tell me the truth or buzz off. I don't want to be around someone who's hiding something from me." Skyler looked self-conscious and seemed about to say more. He closed his mouth without following through, and I figured the jig was up. He must be ready to ditch me. I decided to make it easy on him. "Just because I kissed you once doesn't mean you have to be nice to me," I snarled.

"But I was nice to you before you kissed me," he looked surprised and hurt. *That's true!* I thought. Although I was rude and dismissive of Skyler when we met, he'd stuck with me unwaveringly.

"If I don't kiss you again, will you still like me?"

"Sure, I consider you my friend. I think you would know that, given that we eat lunch and walk home together every day." Skyler always seemed to say all the right things. Still, I struggled. I wasn't sure if I wanted him as a platonic friend or something more, or maybe nothing at all. Sometimes, I wanted to have sex with him, ditch him, and be done with it. Sometimes, his committed Christian streak tempted me to seduce him. That, and the fact I knew he was a virgin. I wondered how it would feel to deflower him, embodying and embracing the Jezebel that many in our community believed me to be.

"What does your mother say about seeing me?" I probed.

"Why do you ask?"

"I'm not stupid. I know you rush down your driveway when your mother's home and pretend we weren't together. If she's gone, you hang out or walk me home. How do you think it feels when you only talk to me at the bus stop, then pretend I'm a stranger while practically running away from me?"

Looking chagrined, Skyler said, "I'm sorry, I know that must not feel nice. To tell the truth, my mother still doesn't want me to see you. But I don't care. She's biased and self-absorbed. If she knew you, she'd change her mind."

"I don't want to stand between you and your mother," I

said calmly. I couldn't blame him for having a family. And, without a mother engaged in my life, I couldn't comprehend Skyler's overbearing one.

"Mom wants me to date her friend's daughter," he finally admitted what was on his mind.

"Who?"

"Do you know Kirsten Jones? She's a junior." Ouch! An adorable, popular cheerleader. Skyler's mom would never accept me in a million years. I already knew that, but hearing her wishes for her son aloud hurt me more than I cared to admit.

"She's a skinny little bitch, like you," I reacted angrily. "So, what? Are you finished with me? Tired of the school tramp?" I couldn't stop mocking, "Skyler and Kirsten, what a cute couple! I can totally see you with her at the prom. That should make Mommy happy."

"My mother is my problem, not yours. If I stopped hanging out with you and dated Kirsten, she'd find another reason to ostracize me," he said, unfazed by my meanness.

"If you want to see Kirsten, I'm not stopping you. Go ahead. It's your life!"

"That's not what I want to do," he remained unruffled.

"I won't be offended if it *is* what you want to do. Rejection doesn't affect me, you know. I've been discarded plenty of times. Long ago, I stopped trying to please anyone else. I'm content to be alone."

"I'm not rejecting you, and I'm not leaving you, Chelsea," said Skyler. Even though he looked and sounded sincere, I couldn't figure out if it was safe to continue trusting him. It frustrated me. I knew he kept the secrets I shared during our interlude in the woods. No word reached me through our asshole classmates. They'd have enjoyed a field day with the details of my shame.

As our shoes crunched down the quiet lane, I recalled that day under the canopy of white pines. When I kissed him, I knew my breasts were in his face, dangling temptingly. Yet he didn't grope me, like every other boy who'd gotten within arm's distance of my body.

"Just because we kissed doesn't mean you need to be my friend," I said more peacefully this time. "If you want to change your mind, I get that. If you want to date Kirsten, no hard feelings," I reiterated my offer of an escape route.

"If you'll have me, I'm sticking with you," he pledged. A little glow ignited in my heart, but my skepticism refused to snuff out. When we reached my house, I stopped and faced him.

"If you promise to behave yourself, I'll show you another secret in my enchanted forest," I bargained. Skyler looked at me curiously.

"Sure, I'd like that," he accepted. I dropped my things inside and discovered Mom napping on the sofa. Quietly, I left her a note in the kitchen and returned to Skyler after locking the front door behind me. He tucked his backpack under the rotting porch floorboards. We reached simultaneously for each other's hand.

Since our last walk, the first frost had fallen on the field behind the house. Although the goldenrod plants remained standing, the grasses were brown and matted down. The air was spicy with the smell of overripe apples and decaying vegetation. The meadow might as well have been a romantic backdrop in some Hollywood movie on a crisp autumn afternoon. As we entered the woodlot, the pathway narrowed. I dropped his hand to walk single file.

"Do you remember this place?" I asked.

"Yes," he affirmed, pointing to our tall tree. "Right there is where you kissed me on the bed of pine needles."

"I'm impressed you remembered," the glow in my heart flared stubbornly.

"You and the white pines are magical."

"Flattery won't get you anywhere with me. We're not having sex," I announced my boundary.

Skyler looked at me quizzically and asked, "Who said anything about sex?"

"All teenage boys have sexual fantasies all the time," I stated matter-of-factly, then wondered, *am I saying that for his benefit or mine?* This strange boy tempted me more than I liked to admit. *It's my senior year,* I reminded myself. *No distractions! No more sex! I want to graduate, get the hell out of here, and start a new life.*

"I suppose you're right," Skyler drawled. I wondered whether he knew that teenage girls had sexual thoughts, too. *Why do I have sex on the brain?* The more I was around Skyler, the hornier I got. But I wasn't about to tell him that!

"We're not dating either," I raised another warning.

"No, this isn't a date. Not at all," he quipped satirically. "We're just holding hands and walking in a deep, dark, secluded forest." I laughed from my gut at his quick-witted comeback. I pointed in the direction I planned to take him.

"The trail gets steep down there. Don't slip," I cautioned, conscious that he still wasn't wholly comfortable in the wild, natural setting of my family's woodlot.

We started hiking down a ravine. Around us, the woods transitioned from the pine canopy into a stand of rich, black-green hemlock trees. As far as I was concerned, this was the most sacred grove on our land. Skyler appeared stunned by the beauty of the ancient forest. I let him absorb it in silence, preoccupied with my downward-spiraling thoughts.

Dozens of times in recent weeks, I'd fantasized about

the way that jerk on the bus's head rolled after I smacked him. For some reason, that memory was haunting me this afternoon. I liked the way it felt. I liked the powerful rush when he slumped, seemingly lifeless.

What should I do with this boy? My thoughts meandered. *Skyler is so weird and innocent. Should I attack him? Slap him again? Punch him hard in his delicate, girlish face?* The nearest house was mine; we were miles from nowhere. No one would ever know if I hit him, even if he yelled. *He's a boy. They're all worthless dickheads!* With a sigh, I acknowledged my problem in this scenario. Skyler *wasn't* a dickhead. He didn't deserve to be roughed up. He was kind and trusting, and trustworthy...so far.

"The hemlocks are incredible," Skyler's gravelly voice, which I loved to hear, broke into my demented train of thought. "I've never seen anything like them."

"I know," I nodded. "It gets better."

We climbed down, down, down into the ravine. *Boys abuse me*; my menacing meditations reared their ugly heads again. *Now it's my turn!* I flirted with the idea of teasing Skyler, humiliating him. I knew how his body reacted when it was pressed up against mine. I weighed whether I should tempt and taunt him by saying no while my body demanded a yes. Physically, I had the upper hand. I felt no qualms in that regard; I could dominate Skyler's slight figure without breaking a sweat. Revenge swayed in my mind's eye like a low-hanging fruit. *Why shouldn't I take advantage of a boy?* In time with my steps, I began to chant silently, 'cunt, cunt, you're a dumb cunt.'

Skyler and I descended deeper into the gloaming of my enchanted forest. My thoughts veered in a new direction. The idea of using Skyler and dumping him afterward intrigued me. This scenario was also a source of my fantasies in the past few weeks. Fuck him with no feelings involved. Cut off this dangerous emotional involvement with a definitive, 'wham, bam, thank you, ma'am.' I knew my problem with this scenario was that if I had sex with Skyler and dumped him, I would regret the loss of his presence in my daily life. I felt the glow in my heart guttering under the shadowy weight of these impure, cruel visions.

"You're quiet," Skyler stopped to rest on the side of the crude path and faced me. We breathed heavily from the exertion. "What are you thinking about?" I almost laughed, imagining the comical expression on his face if I admitted the truth.

"Nothing, except enjoying that you appreciate what I appreciate," I told a half-truth. Skyler's pretty face lit up. "Come on, there's still a way to go."

This part of the trek was steeper and rockier; we slowed to a crawl to pick our way further to the bottom of the ravine. I decided before we moved very far downhill. *At my mother's next psych appointment, I'm leaving her in the waiting room and taking her time slot.* Accepting that I needed help was hard, but I convinced myself. *Mom's sick, as always—nothing new there. Clearly, something's off with me. I've got to talk to someone.*

I recalled a night the week before when Dad was preparing to leave for the graveyard shift. I overheard him and Mom talking behind their closed bedroom door. He was trying to communicate to her that he may lose his job and that we may need to move. I didn't want to be forced to leave my only home to finish my senior year in another part of the state. I didn't want to leave my only friend.

Arriving at the bottom of the ravine, we halted along a narrow ridge. A few yards to the north was a marsh. We turned to study the steep gorge we'd descended to reach where we now stood. Looking up, we couldn't see the top of the massive, towering hemlock tree above us.

"Come on, we're almost there," I reclaimed Skyler's hand now that we could walk two abreast. We made our way to the base of the magnificent forest giant in the primordial setting. We settled to the ground together.

"What do you think?" I asked softly.

"Beautiful! Hemlocks are amazing," he said with reverence, staring upward. I tightened my grip on his hand and snuggled next to him, relieved that he appreciated my favorite place on earth. My sanctuary. It was where I found relief from the heat of summer and respite from the frigid, falling snow of winter. My hemlock rose tall and strong, her sensual body swaying but remaining resilient as she endured the onslaught of the seasons year after year.

"Let's sit for a few minutes," I whispered. Skyler nodded, still gazing heavenward.

Even when the sun shone bright, little light pierced this deep into the sylvan underbelly of the forest. My senses were sharp. I listened to my hemlock, her evergreen needles swishing in a light breeze. A pair of chickadees danced on a limb in search of her seeds. High in a distant white oak tree on the side of the slope, a squirrel scampered with an acorn. A warm feeling of peace and contentment passed through me.

I put a hand on Skyler's shoulder and guided him beside me onto his back. I swung my leg over his waist and nestled into his chest like a pillow. Curled around his body, without a word, I held on for the longest time. I kissed him on the lips, far gentler than last time. I stroked his forehead. With my finger, I closed his eyelids. I closed mine, too. We nuzzled together under the protection of our ancient hemlock tree.

In the shadow of the ravine, as the midafternoon air turned cooler, I felt warm. I felt secure. I felt safe. I fell into a solid, heavy sleep.

Sometime later, Skyler rubbed my back and rocked my hips with his. I gradually opened my eyes. It was the deepest I'd slept in months. Maybe years! Although the light was still visible in the western sky, twilight descended within the hemlock forest.

"Why'd you let me sleep so long?" I sat up.

"You were zonked out. You needed to sleep."

"It's way past dinnertime. Mom will be so worried," I fretted. "And you're going to get into deep trouble!"

"I don't mind. It felt good to be held. Felt good to hold you. I felt trusted," he said sincerely.

"I did—I mean, I do trust you," I affirmed, realizing that I'd slept with a boy for the first time...slept without having sex. Skyler was different. Perhaps with Skyler, I was different, too.

We brushed away the deep green hemlock needles that clung to our clothes. In near darkness, we carefully climbed out of the ravine. I could barely see the path, and owls began to hoot around us. Walking through the woodlot and field, we held hands while we practiced our speeches to our mothers.

CHAPTER 7
DISCONTENT
SKYLER

December

On the first Thursday in December, Chelsea emerged from her house after school with a wool blanket draped over her shoulder. That was the signal we were going to be walking in the woods for some time. We ventured past the pine grove and scurried down the ravine to the hemlock forest. Reaching our special hemlock giant, Chelsea rolled out the blanket, sat down, and patted the space beside her. I sat, too.

"Skyler, we need to talk," she said in a gloomy tone. My heart sank. "Typically, my father works fifty or more hours a week at the tool and die shop. Last month, his hours decreased each week. His company is shifting more work to their renovated plant in Detroit. Unfortunately, Dad may need to transfer to metro Detroit to keep his job."

"Not good," I responded guardedly. "What are the implications for you?"

"If his plant closes, we'll be moving."

It took a minute for me to master my emotional reaction.

"Can you at least finish the year at our school?" I asked.

"If Dad's transferred, he'll take Mom with him. If she goes, I have to go. Nothing is certain yet, but I wanted to give you a heads-up." Silence fell between us.

"What a paradox for you and me," I finally said. "After finding friendship, we'll be separated."

"Skyler, life is unpredictable. Doors open and close beyond our control. Let's enjoy the time we have together," Chelsea said philosophically. While I knew she was right to adopt this attitude, I didn't want any part in it. I wanted my friend! Chelsea had grown more important to me with every passing day.

We kissed briefly, stretched out on the blanket, and snuggled together. I saw the signs I'd come to recognize. With the extreme strain of caring for her mother and the uncertainty in her life, I knew Chelsea cherished the quiet hours we spent together. She needed a friend. She needed to rest. Within a few minutes, she fell asleep.

Due to the onset of winter, I couldn't let Chelsea sleep too late into the afternoon. At 4:30, I licked her neck and ear. We barely managed to climb out of the ravine before the 5:00 sunset.

By mid-December, I sensed our relationship changing. Incrementally, my friend withdrew from me more each day. Rationally, I understood; she was protecting herself from the impending doom of relocation. I recognized that her behavior was not a personal reflection on me. I supported her as best I could and spent as much time with her as she allowed. At the same time, I was dejected. I tried to hide my despondency.

Our school term ended on the Thursday before Christmas. Chelsea suggested we stop at my house as we exited the bus. She said I needed to change into something warmer and get my hiking boots before we walked into the snow-covered woods. I invited her to step inside my house. My mother was home early from work.

"Mom, this is Chelsea. Chelsea, this is my mother," I introduced them to each other.

"Hello, Chelsea," Mom said coldly.

"Pleasure to finally meet you," said Chelsea politely, extending her hand. My mother did not shake it. She turned away and resumed frosting cookies for the Christmas Eve school bake sale without a word.

"Mom, I'm putting on my hiking clothes," I ignored her bad manners, even though I wanted to call her out for her un-Christian reception of my friend. "We're going for a walk."

"There's a dangerous winter weather warning. Walk her home and get back here immediately," she jerked her head in Chelsea's direction and looked grim.

"We'll be fine," I refused to bend to her will. "The forest protects us from blizzards, and we know our way in the woods. I'll be back in a few hours," I motioned for Chelsea to follow me to my bedroom. I closed the door.

As Chelsea watched me change, she smiled and giggled. There was a girl in my bedroom for the first time in my life. She filled my room with color. She was delightful. Enchanting. I regretted not inviting her over sooner!

After I pulled on my winter gear, we headed out. I didn't bother saying goodbye to Mommy Dearest, whom I could hear banging baking trays in the kitchen over the din of the evening news. I knew her foul mood was partly due to the call she received from my father last night when he informed her that he would not be home for Christmas this year.

Stepping outside, the snow pelted our faces. We walked arm in arm to the safety of Chelsea's place. Once there, she reciprocated and invited me inside.

"Mom," said Chelsea. "This is the boy I mentioned to you. Skyler, I want you to meet my mother."

"Hello," I shook her hand. We smiled at each other.

"I've heard everything about you, Skyler. Chelsea says you're a true friend," she said pleasantly. Contrary to all the rumors, Chelsea's mom was not scary. Although she was pale, I couldn't detect any signs of mental illness. I noticed the place was tidier than on the first day of school when I innocently followed Chelsea home and found her in her bra and panties. Also, a pile of collapsed cardboard boxes sat in the corner, and six rolls of packing tape were stacked neatly on a baker's shelf.

"We're hiking into the ravine," Chelsea said.

"Nothing compares to the pristine beauty of the hemlock forest blanketed in two feet of snow. Chelsea knows the way with her eyes closed," she smiled at me and then looked proudly at her daughter. "When you get back, you'll be chilled to the bone, and I'll make hot chocolate."

Once outside, we grabbed each other's mittened hands and traipsed through the deep snowdrifts in the field. Upon reaching the forest, I was gob-smacked. The place had come wonderfully alive. With each gust of wind, great tree branches swayed and creaked. High above us, the sentinels battled the gale force blizzard for survival. Below where we walked arm in arm, the white pines and hemlocks provided shelter from the storm. Chelsea cast our blanket on the snow-dusted woodland floor, the same as always. We embraced and kissed. We watched and listened to the wind roaring through the tree limbs high over our heads.

"Our hours in my enchanted forest are numbered," she whispered against my chilly cheek. "By the time the winter snow drifts make the ravine impassable, I'll be long gone."

"Oh, no. Please don't tell me," I moaned.

"Next week, we're moving four hours away to the eastern side of the state," she delivered the death blow.

"What about us?"

"Today is the last time I'll see you for a long time," she answered mournfully. "Next year, you'll go off to your private out-of-state university. My grades suck. I'll be lucky to be accepted at a community college. Wish I could move out, but Dad wants me to live at home to help with mom," she revealed her plan.

"Can I at least call you?"

"Of course! If you need to talk, call me. I'll always answer. I'll always be your friend," she said in a non-Chelsea-like animated voice.

"Will I ever see you again?"

"That'll be difficult, Skyler, and you know it. We'll be a thousand miles apart, literally and figuratively. Even though we're good for each other, we will be separated."

"Let's make a pact," I was desperate not to lose her. "After college, after we have jobs and money, let's meet."

"Sounds like a good plan. In the meantime, keep a journal. We can compare notes."

"I'll miss you. I'll miss our journeys into the woods," I said.

"Me, too. My dad may need to sell the house, but he plans to keep some of the property, including the pine woodlot and the hemlock forest."

"Let's pledge to return to these woods together someday!"

"Skyler, you're an incurable romantic," she laughed. "What did I do to deserve you? I love you. Whatever happens in your life, wherever you go, remember, once upon a time, you were loved."

The wind picked up. We folded our blanket and headed out of the forest. I stomped the snow off my boots at Chelsea's house and stood by the hot wood stove. As promised, her mom handed each of us a steaming cup of hot chocolate before wishing me goodbye. She blew Chelsea a kiss before slipping into the security of her bedroom. After we drank our cocoa, Chelsea hugged me and escorted me to the door.

"Skyler, remember the first time we met? I pushed you away. I was afraid to care about anyone or anything. Yet, you didn't give up on me. You persevered and became my only friend. I'll never forget you," she said tearfully.

I fought back my own tears to say, "You changed me, Chelsea. I'll never be the same person. You opened my eyes. You liberated me." I stifled a sob and apologized, "I'm sorry; I don't want to say goodbye."

"We must move forward. No turning back. Don't hibernate this winter. Promise me you'll start seeing another girl. Be courageous; ask Kirsten on a date," coached my friend. "You can't judge her based on her looks or her parents. Every girl has a story. Maybe she'll surprise you. Maybe she'll be nice."

"I only want to be with you," I protested.

Chelsea blinked several times, tilted her head, and sighed, "You're too sweet. Run along, now. The drifts are getting high on the road," she pulled open the door. "Oh, one more piece of advice from your friend," she added

brightly. "Don't let the so-called Christians at school oblit-
erate your soul. Never abandon your faith; it makes you so
special. Thank you for everything, Skyler," she embraced
me one final time.

Like the day we met, she nudged me out the door and
onto the front porch of the old yellow farmhouse. For the
last time, our lips met. Hers were warm and wet.

"Goodbye, Chelsea," I said. Stepping off the porch,
hoping for one last look, I turned. She was gone.

CHAPTER 8
SEPARATION
SKYLER

January

On a Tuesday, after I stepped off the bus, I did not turn my feet toward home. I walked down the icy gravel road. An unseen force propelled me to Chelsea's house. I fantasized that she'd be there. Stepping onto her porch, I knocked on the door.

Only silence greeted me.

I knocked again, though I knew no answer was forthcoming. The door swung open silently. I entered the desolate space. On the ground floor, I examined four small rooms. The living room was trashed; old, torn cushions from a sofa were scattered about. A few dirty dishes festered, forgotten in the kitchen sink. The bathroom was filthy. I spied a bloody towel on the floor in the corner.

Although I was afraid, I walked into her mother's bedroom. Grimy sheets lay in a heap on an abandoned, stained mattress. The stench of urine rose from the pile. I felt sorry for Chelsea.

I walked up a narrow staircase to a small bedroom on the second level. Under the steep pitch of the ceiling, I could barely stand up straight. Chelsea's strawberry fragrance lingered in the room; I closed my eyes and breathed her aroma deeply. Unlike the other rooms, her space was swept clean. All the furniture was gone except for a heavy old wooden sailor's chest. Kneeling, I opened the lid.

A few random items lined the bottom of the box. A scratched antique doll clothed with a few scraps of linen. An emerald-green sweater sized for a first- or second-grade schoolgirl. A tattered journal. I pulled it out and read a few lines:

> *The swamp near the giant hemlock is*
>   *teeming with life.*
> *Skunk cabbage is up.*
> *The marsh marigolds are blossoming.*
> *Little rivulets of water meander through last*
>   *year's old sedges.*
> *I heard a frog.*
> *I wish I could skip school!*
> *I wish I could stay in the woods all day.*
> *Tomorrow, I shall return to the swamp.*
> *Tomorrow, I shall take off my shoes and walk*
>   *in the marsh.*

I tucked the doll, sweater, and journal under my jacket before taking one last look around the room. I descended the rickety staircase and walked home. I missed my

Chelsea! If we weren't lovers, why was I lost without her? I admired her bold, brassy personality. I admired the strength she developed from years of hardship and pain. Underneath her rough exterior, she was soft. She liked me. She was gone.

CHAPTER 9
BETRAYAL
SKYLER

February

Alone again in my room after school, I heard my mother's cell phone ring. When her voice reached me, I kicked open my bedroom door to eavesdrop. I'd been reduced to this unseemly vicarious social interaction in the absence of my only friend.

"What a coincidence! My husband is out of town on business, too. Skyler and I look forward to dinner with you and Kirsten," the dreaded family dinner date was finally slated to happen. Somehow, my mother hadn't managed to force it to take place last fall when she first threatened. Her work on the Financial Assistance Committee and her push to win the race for a school board seat in the upcoming election had swallowed most of her free time. I couldn't help but think that Chelsea's relocation cooled her fever to force Kirsten and me into couplehood.

On cue, Mom said, "You heard correctly," her voice

dropped an octave as though she were speaking of someone who'd recently passed. "Chelsea and her family moved out over a month ago. Alyssa, I prayed for them every day! God answers prayers. A fresh start will be healthy for them. I truly wish them well," she said reverently. A brief pause ensued.

"Relieved? Certainly, I can breathe again with the threat removed," Mom heaved an exaggerated sigh. She quickly added, "Mind you, Skyler and Chelsea were only friends. Among all the lovely girls at school, why he chose to hang out with a lost cause, I'll never know." Exiting my room, I snuck downstairs, moving closer to overhear the conversation better.

"Baggage is an understatement," Mom agreed. "I'm not blaming her, you know. Chelsea was traumatized. Can you imagine? Her mother was a basket case." I was nearby enough to discern the tinny, shrill voice of Mrs. Jones but not near enough to make out her words.

When Mom announced, "Alyssa, I'm cooking. Let me put you on speaker," I wondered if God had answered my unspoken prayer. "Can you hear me now?"

"Loud and clear, Francine," replied Mrs. Jones. I was treated to both ends of the conversation with the speaker on high volume.

"Well," my mother took back the baton. "If only half the rumors were true, Chelsea didn't belong with us."

"Sometimes our Christian charity backfires on us," Mrs. Jones sermonized. "You're aware, aren't you, that committee members approved Chelsea's scholarship without being alerted to her, shall we say, permissive history? She was presented as a special case under the protection of the prior chair of the Financial Assistance Committee. He was appallingly lax in matters of this kind."

"I'll say," agreed my mother. "He absolutely failed in his due diligence. It's scandalous, but now we know not to let it happen again." I wanted to strangle her for her ignorant rumormongering, but I kept quiet in my hidden alcove at the foot of the stairs.

"This is exactly why I'm so glad you arrived and took over, Francine. A risqué girl like that had no business attending our school, no matter how compelling and tragic the case her father made to the former chairperson. Although we deeply feel our Christian sympathies, we must stand on guard to protect our daughters from being exposed to girls with loose morals."

"I couldn't agree more, Alyssa. Chelsea was too mature and hedonistic to be around the virtuous, god-fearing children attending our schools. I worried about her influence on the boys, too," Mom piled smears on rumors.

"To call her a bad influence is an understatement. It was obvious that Chelsea couldn't control herself with boys or her diet," sneered Mrs. Jones. Just then, Mom caught a glimpse of me at the bottom of the staircase. Her face turned ashen when the realization hit that I'd overheard everything. She froze. I turned my back and mounted the stairs. Behind me, I heard her friend calling, "Francine? Are you still there?"

"Yes, Alyssa, I'm with you," Mom said in a strained voice.

"I thought I lost you," Mrs. Jones laughed. "In any case, it's time for me to go. See you tomorrow for dinner at our place. Kirsten and I have already planned the menu, so don't bring anything. Well, don't bring anything except your boy, Skyler."

"We'll see you then," Mom confirmed and ended the call.

CHAPTER 10
NORMAL
SKYLER

The Next Day

n the spirit of honoring my promise to Chelsea, I went to the Jones' house for dinner with my mother. But for that promise, I'd never have complied when Mom announced, "Time to go, Skyler. Let's enjoy ourselves, and please remember your manners when speaking to Mrs. Jones. She isn't used to your sullen attitude like I am."

During dinner, the moms made small talk. They chatted about their family histories and pressured Kirsten and me to join the conversation. As their discussion shifted to school matters, they began asking for our opinions on various teachers. I felt trapped, hounded by a double dose of motherly attention. Plus, being around Kirsten made me anxious. She was the queen bee of the popular kids' group and flawlessly drop-dead gorgeous. In my nervousness, I could only sneak intermittent peeks at her. She appeared as uncomfortable as I felt with the dinner scene. After we finished the meal, the moms rose and moved toward the kitchen in a clearly coordinated ploy for Kirsten and me to strike up a friendship.

Carrying a large stack of dirty dishes, Mrs. Jones said with a sickly-sweet smile, "Kids, you don't need to help. We'll be cleaning and chatting in the kitchen. I'm sure you have lots to talk about, too." Mom nodded her enthusiastic support and hurried her friend through the swinging door.

When they were finally out of sight, Kirsten hissed, "Skyler, let's get out of here. My mother is driving me nuts!"

"I'm game," I was thankful she'd broken the ice. "They're so obvious, trying to push us together. It's painful." Kirsten nodded and went to crack the kitchen door.

"Mom, I'm going to give Skyler a tour," she said. "We'll hang out in the pole barn until time for dessert." I could hear both moms' giddy encouragement of her escape plan.

As I walked with Kirsten through the large house and cavernous garage, I studied her up close. She seemed cool. At least she treated me like we were almost already friends. I couldn't help but admire her body, which was slender with a flat chest. It was the opposite of Chelsea's. The contrast struck me. And she looked so young compared to Chelsea! Chelsea appeared to be a mature woman at nineteen; just a year and a half younger, Kirsten looked like a fourteen-year-old with long, straight, bleached platinum blonde hair. In the pole barn, my hostess paused to flip an electrical switch. Huge overhead fluorescent lights illuminated a basketball court and reflected in her grey eyes like flecks of silver glitter.

"Do you play?" she asked.

"Only a little," I admitted, nerves twinging again.

"Let's go one-on-one, just for fun," she challenged. I was impressed by her graceful, practiced form on the court. Her sleek body glided around me, hitting two baskets for every one of mine.

"You lose, I win," she boasted when she hit 30. Before I could retort, she said, "Come on, I want to show you our game room." It shocked me when she took my hand in hers.

Leading me to the far end of the pole barn, she opened the door to a smaller, enclosed room. It was filled with a big-screen TV, a card table, and an oversized black leather sectional couch. Kirsten squeezed my hand and drew me inside. She shut the door, bolted it behind us in a flash, and flattened herself against a wall. Except for a thin ray of light streaming around the edge of a curtain on a small window, the room was entirely dark.

"Come here," she commanded, yanking me close to kiss me hard. Instinctively, I kissed back. Her breathing was heavy. After a short embrace, she pulled away. In the dim light, I saw her grab the hem of her shirt and yank it over her head, exposing what appeared to be a black silk bra trimmed in lace. Dumbfounded, I didn't move.

"What's the matter?" she murmured before pulling me against her lean body. "Aren't you going to unsnap my bra?" Still in shock, I sprang into action, fumbling to undo the clasp between her shoulder blades. Beneath it, I felt warm perspiration slicking her smooth skin. When the undergarment fell to the floor, and I didn't do more, she said, "Aren't you going to feel me up?" I stood mute against her, uncertain how to proceed. "Do you need my permission? Go ahead, touch me," Kirsten urged and pressed one of my hands against a tiny, tight breast. I massaged gently. With a moan, she wedged her narrow thigh into my crotch. She began humping my leg, chest rising and falling rhythmically.

"I'm getting hot," she whispered before unfastening the

button at the top of her jeans. Still dazed, I didn't recipro-cate beyond holding her against me and fondling her breast. After a few seconds, she stopped and asked impatiently, "What's your problem, Skyler?" I decided I better do some-thing to avoid a conflict. So, I placed my hand on her belly, inside the open fly of her jeans but over the black silk panties that matched her discarded bra. I pressed against her lower abdomen, wondering about her expectations.

"You're afraid," she exclaimed. "I thought you were experienced!" I slipped my hand around to the small of her back and pulled her body closer to mine. "Not there," she snapped. She grabbed my hand roughly to guide it back to the front, inside her underwear, and then downward.

"Oh, you're making me wet," she moaned. I tried to withdraw my hand. "Stay there. It's good," she whispered. I complied until I felt her pelvis begin to pulsate. Still doubt-ful, I moved to pull out my hand.

"No," she snapped. "Don't stop now, moron," she thrust her vulva firmly against my entrapped hand and rubbed. "I'm cumming! I'm cumming!" she cried, body jerking under my grasp. I held perfectly still while my thoughts spiraled. After the longest time, Kirsten's body relaxed. She pulled me down to the couch, squeezed me, and laughed exuberantly.

"This was your first time! I can tell. Have you ever kissed a girl before?" I didn't answer. "For sure, you've never touched a girl. Ever give a girl an orgasm?" I still didn't answer. "You had no idea what you were doing," she taunted in an off-putting, haughty voice. "At school, everyone said you had sex with Chelsea. I guess she wasn't orgasmic!"

"We did not have sex," I managed to speak. "I love Chelsea."

"You made a big mistake by hanging out with her. That was a major no-no. Everyone knows she's a lying, manipulative slut." I didn't like where this conversation was going but I maintained my calm. I'd had plenty of practice with my mother.

"Not true. Chelsea was misunderstood," I stuck up for my friend.

"Whatever," Kirsten waved dismissively. "We're all glad she moved. I say, good riddance," she paused, seemingly waiting for me to join in her condemnation of Chelsea. When I didn't, she changed the subject.

"Next time we do this, I'll have to teach you how to pleasure me properly. By the way," her tone turned threatening. "You better not talk about what happened between us. Because, if you do, I'll tell everyone you're a virgin. And that you couldn't manage to have sex with Chelsea, the school slut. And that you were afraid to touch me!"

"I wasn't afraid," I finally found my voice. "I was shocked, Kirsten. I only came to your house tonight because my mother insisted. She wants us to be friends."

"Friends?" she laughed scornfully. "Yeah, that's not happening. I didn't want to spend time with you either, you know. I told my mom you were a geek, but she's all in love with your mom. She forced me to come to dinner. I got even with her, didn't I? If she'd caught us together, you'd be in big trouble!" Like quicksilver, her tone shifted again. She sounded jealous when she asked, "Did you like being with a flat-chested girl like me, or were you mesmerized by Chelsea's big tits?"

My head spun. I didn't know how to respond. Everything with Kirsten moved fast! I didn't know her. What was she doing with me? Was she playing me? Using me? It was impossible to tell. I felt a little nauseated. Kirsten huffed and stood up, abandoning me on the big black sofa. When she turned on the lights, I was dazzled by her beauty. I watched her snap on her tiny black bra, slip her T-shirt over her silken black hair, and zip her jeans.

She faced me and said imperiously, "This little rendezvous is our secret. If you say you were at my house, I'll deny it," she laughed. "Sorry, no offense. Nobody would believe I kissed a dork."

"That's rude," I interjected.

"Not rude. Honest," Kirsten corrected me, then began to outline her expectations. "Here are the rules. One, I can't talk to you at school. You understand. Nothing personal. Okay?"

"Can you give me one reason why we can't be friends at school?" I struggled to understand the bewildering scenario.

"Everyone thinks you're weird," she said bluntly. "I'm normal. You're not. I can't risk losing my friends, so I can't be your friend in public. And no one can know we've been together."

"Explain normal and weird."

"Trust me, you don't want to know," she warned. "I'm sick of this scene. Let's go back to the house."

"Not before you tell me the truth," I stood and blocked the door.

"Okay, but the truth hurts," she crossed her arms over her chest. "First, every day, you sat with Chelsea in the cafeteria. She wasn't one of us. That makes you a weirdo and a loser. Second, everyone thinks you're a girl. Or a wannabe girl. Not normal," she said in a high satirical voice.

"Girl?" I wanted clarification.

"You look and act like a girl, Skyler, in case you haven't noticed! Everything about you screams female."

"Tell me more about what people think," I seized the

opportunity to understand better where I stood with my peers. She looked skeptical. "You can be brutally honest. It's not the first time I've heard comments like this."

"Fine. Isn't it obvious? You're short for a guy, small-boned, and you have that girlish face. Half the time, you wear your hair in a ponytail. What guy does that?" she eyed me askance. "Sitting across from you at the dinner table tonight, I could've been looking at my reflection in a mirror. You could pass for my twisted twin sister."

"Am I as pretty as you?" I asked, half in jest.

"I might even say prettier. You ooze femininity. You're soft and gentle like a girl. And earlier, you proved my point when you wouldn't take me," she rolled her eyes.

"Take you?" I keyed in on the phrase.

"You didn't even try to have sex with me."

"Was I supposed to pressure you to have sex?"

"I threw myself at you! You could've taken me," there was that phrase again. "I had to show you what to do when you could've dominated me. That's not how real guys act," Kirsten critiqued brutally.

"If your friends think I'm weird, why were you even nice to me tonight?"

"I told you already," she replied impatiently. "To get back at my mother because she made me have dinner with you. Can't you see? My mother wants to impress your mother. More like, use your mother."

"But *you* think I'm abnormal," I pointed out. "Using me to get back at your mother when you feel that way about me is totally contradictory."

"Well, it wasn't my *only* reason for touching you. I wanted to know if you're a boy or a girl," she sniggered.

"That's not funny," I said flatly.

"I'm sorry, Skyler. Really, I am," her tone shifted but

wasn't fully sincere or aligned with her words. "I'm teasing. I like you—a little. You're sensitive and girly. I wish you *were* a girl," I was surprised to hear her repeat what Chelsea said early on in our acquaintance. "I like you, but I can't be seen with you," she finished on a derisive note.

Frustrated at my lack of understanding of the high school social parameters by which Kirsten lived, I asked, "Why, exactly, can't you be seen with me?"

"Why do I have to be so explicit with you?" Kirsten rolled her eyes again. "In class, you talked about LGBT rights. You defended *those people!* Did you forget we go to a Christian school, Skyler? Gays and lesbians aren't accepted in our community. Homosexuality is against the law of God. You may not be gay, but you're queer, which is close enough. I can't be seen with you," she repeated. I recognized the fear in Kirsten. She, unlike Chelsea and me, hadn't been ostracized before. Kirsten lived in a world where anyone 'other' to her was scary and represented a threat to the small corner of the world she inhabited. I'd lived in a world like that recently.

"So, what am I supposed to do?" I spoke respectfully, wanting to be clear on the rules she clung to so desperately. She seemed relieved that she'd finally gotten through to me.

"Don't talk to me at school. Don't look at me in the hallways," she enumerated on her fingers. "Don't text me. Don't call me."

"This is strange," I reflected aloud. "I'm not sure I like this deal. What are we to each other?"

She surprised me with a devilish grin and said, "You're my boy toy, you idiot. My secret playmate. I'm your mysterious, incredibly sexy, popular, private, exclusive, elusive, silent goddess." She sounded anxious when she asked, "You like me, right? Want to be with me?"

"I find you intriguing," I admitted. "Are you my femme fatale?" Kirsten gratified me by laughing wholeheartedly at my joke.

"You're clever," she complimented. "And you make me laugh. If you tell anyone about us, you'll be finished."

"So, how will this work? You and me?"

"If my mom's out for the night, I may invite you over to keep me company. Mom's highly protective; she rarely lets me stay home alone," she complained. Then she made a frightened face and said, "Plus, I get scared." I believed her; the look was not feigned.

"Won't your mom be suspicious?"

"No. My mom knows you're not my type," Kirsten's bluntness reappeared. "I'd never go out with someone like you." The entire arrangement simultaneously disgusted and intrigued me, but I found myself willing to be her accomplice. There was no denying her charm or her cunning. Chelsea's voice rang in my ears, reminding me that I'd be off to college next year. I didn't care what my classmates thought of me while I remained here; I'd long ago given up that burden. I remembered Chelsea's plea, too. She coached me to give Kirsten a chance. Here was that chance, unlooked for but not unwelcome. I smiled and nodded at my new illicit acquaintance.

"What's the deal with our mothers, anyway?" I asked while I had her attention. She looked at me pityingly.

"Your mother is popular, Skyler. Everyone likes her. My mom thinks she's cool. My mom told me, for her sake, we can't completely ignore you," Kirsten said in a logical voice.

"How do you think that makes me feel?"

"What you *should* feel is grateful that I'm spending one second with you," she deflected and, confusingly, winked at me. "Let's get back in the house. Time to eat dessert."

To my mind, Kirsten *was* the tantalizing dessert. Even before she revealed just how little liked I was at school, I knew she was out of my league. I'd never talked with a pretty, in-crowd girl. Let alone been touched by one. Since Chelsea left, I was desperately alone at school, after school, and at home. I craved companionship. I craved being touched.

I craved Kirsten.

If Chelsea could see me, I knew she would tell me to be true to myself. The only problem was that without Chelsea, I felt unsure of myself. Who was I? Who did I want to be?

CHAPTER 11
RENDEZVOUS
SKYLER

May

Every school day throughout March and April, I watched Kirsten. Between classes or in the cafeteria, my eyes tracked her movements. She flowed effortlessly over the campus with her clique in the junior class. I adored her. She never spoke to me or looked at me that whole time.

Hours, days, and weeks dragged on. Instead of lamenting Chelsea's absence at home after school, I fantasized about Kirsten. I longed to see her. Waiting for Kirsten's call drove me crazy. I asked myself endless questions, wondering if her silence would ever break. When would I see her again? Was our interlude an illusion? Did she change her mind?

At last, during the first week of May, Kirsten called. She invited me to spend the evening at her house. As I arrived at her door, I met her departing mother.

"Oh, Skyler, I'm sorry I didn't see you were standing there," Mrs. Jones startled at my appearance. "Thank you for keeping Kirsten company while I go to this corporate function," she treated me to her usual sickly-sweet smile. "Help yourself to the leftover spaghetti in the refrigerator if you're hungry."

Once inside, Kirsten escorted me to the rec room. As she walked before me, I admired her backside, outlined in loose-fitting, shiny workout shorts. She turned on a movie. Wordlessly, she took my hand and led me to the couch. We sat close together, holding hands. Midway through the show, she leaned into me. We kissed. I placed my hand on her bare thigh. She pushed my hand up and under her shorts, where I discovered she wasn't wearing panties.

"Touch me," she whispered. As we kissed, I obeyed.

"No, not there," she reached down to move my finger to her clitoris. "There. Don't stop," she commanded. She sucked hard on my tongue for a long time as we kissed. Her breathing became heavier and heavier. She pressed her hand on the outside of my pants between my legs. After a scene similar to the last time we were together when she orgasmed, she slid away from me to the other side of the couch. She dismissed me, saying, "I don't want to finish the movie. You can go home now."

Disappointed, I said, "Can we talk?"

"No," she snickered. "Why would I want to talk to you?"

"I told your mother I'd stay till she got home. Don't you want me to stay?"

"No, and I can't see you anymore," Kirsten said enigmatically.

"Did I do something wrong?"

"No, you're fine. You have a soft touch, like a girl," she

laughed a little. "Wish we could do this again. Too bad I can't."

"Why?"

"I have a boyfriend. If he found out you kissed me, he'd pound the ever-loving shit out of you. It's for your protection."

"I waited over a month for you to call, Kirsten! You used me," I accused.

"Don't start crying like a little girl, Skyler. Grow up! You used me, too. I see you watching me everywhere I go at school. I know you fantasize about me every day after school, too," she didn't pull any punches. "Everyone uses everyone else," she shrugged.

THAT NIGHT IN BED AT HOME, I REFLECTED ON MY senior year and the women whose presence by my side had changed me.

Chelsea taught me the impact of trauma, ridicule, and rejection. She was my mysterious, complicated first love.

My relationship with Francine, my overbearing mother, proved I could walk away from convention and maintain a sliver of integrity.

Observing Mrs. Jones, I witnessed a brown-nosing parent willing to sacrifice her family and Christian morals to seek popularity.

With Kirsten, my two-faced secret lover, I lost myself in order to escape isolation and pursue physical intimacy.

At the end of May, I graduated. Although thankful to be alive, I felt ground down and battered by my high school experience. Disillusioned with the world, I built a fortress within to protect myself.

While attending my university's summer orientation, I

visited the career center. Though I hadn't planned to relo-
cate there until the school year started, I accepted the offer
of an immediate job opportunity on campus, working in a
residence hall. Back home, I delivered the news to my
mother, bid her goodbye, and moved out of the house.

PART TWO

CHAPTER 12
ENCOUNTER
SKYLER

Nine Years Later
July

S tanding in line at the Back Country Deli, I heard the bells tinkle and the screen door slam behind me. I turned and stared at the young woman who entered. Organically, I knew she was Janeen. Intuitively, I knew she was The One.

Her thick, jet-black hair was pulled back in a ponytail, sharpening the distinctive features of her olive-skinned face. A face that, without a trace of make-up, was radiant. Her eyes were as black as her inky hair. With naturally dusky lips, she required no lipstick. Her chiseled physique affirmed my intuition if I had any doubt about her identity; this person was a first-class athlete. Her broad shoulders accentuated her narrow waist and hips. A bright white sports bra peeked through the wide neck of her loose-fitting cut-off tee shirt, which exposed her ripped abs. Short silky boxer shorts revealed her muscular thighs.

As I watched her approach, my heart pounded. She didn't acknowledge my presence. I swallowed before attempting to speak with the goddess.

"You must be Janeen," I coughed on my words. She stared through me for several seconds as though she hadn't heard me, then turned to look out the front window. I tried again. "You're Janeen, right?" She revolved to look at me. Her eyes raked my body up and down. An unusually long time passed before she spoke.

"Do I know you?" she asked in a deep, dark, irritated voice.

"No, we've never met."

"Am I supposed to know you?"

"No, I can't think of why you should."

"Then how do you know me?"

"I don't," I shrugged.

"You don't just walk up to a woman and start talking," she criticized. "It's impolite."

"Technically, you walked up to me. It would be impolite if I didn't greet you," I teased lightly.

"Forget politeness. I'm into privacy. What possessed you to speak to me?"

"Fortunately, or perhaps unfortunately since you're into privacy, you're already famous. Everyone's hoping you come to work at the academy. Hello, Janeen. I'm Skyler," I introduced myself. She turned to scan the nearby shelves. Eventually, her eyes swiveled back to where I stood, patiently waiting.

"You've got a lot of nerve," she said. "You're lucky I don't pepper-spray you."

"I'm sorry I startled you."

"Exactly what have you heard about me?"

"You're a volleyball legend."

"So, you work at the academy?" she inferred.

"How did you guess?" I smiled. Janeen took my rhetorical question literally.

"We're in the middle of nowhere," she surmised. "Not many people our age are to be found in this godforsaken wilderness. Therefore, it makes sense that you work for the academy," she returned to scanning the shelves and ignoring me. I stepped to the counter to buy a salami sandwich.

After I collected my meal, I turned to the goddess and said, "Welcome aboard! I look forward to working with you." I extended my hand.

She regarded it suspiciously and said, "Technically, I'm still in limbo. I haven't signed the contract. I'm curious; how did you know I'm considering working at the academy?"

"We're in the middle of nowhere. Not many people our age around. Therefore, I deduced you were considering working at the academy."

"Smart ass," she snarled. I couldn't help but laugh; I felt giddy in her presence.

"Honestly, I heard a rumor last weekend," I admitted. "You're causing quite the stir in our godforsaken wilderness. Pretty hot stuff."

"If that was your attempt to flirt with me, you fell on your face. Get handsy with me, and I'll report you to Grady," she snapped.

"My boss, you mean? Please! Grady would be on my side if I were flirting with you," I bantered, trying to lighten the tone. I was deeply attracted to this gorgeous woman, but she acted like a first-class bitch. "For the record, I wasn't flirting. Don't worry."

"What, me? Worry about you?" she laughed dismissively. "Not a chance! You're obviously not an athlete and no match for me. I can handle you," she planted her feet shoulder-width apart and stood firm.

"No doubt you can take care of yourself," I agreed, allowing my eyes to travel down her solid form.

"Pig! I know exactly what you're doing," she glared.

"What am I doing?"

"Undressing me with your eyes. Typical male!"

"Don't flatter yourself," I advised. "Grady has a knack for recruiting forceful, perky women with chiseled athletic bodies."

Looking scandalized, she insisted, "Stop now, or I'll have you fired."

"It's the middle of summer," I told her, put off by her fullness of self. "Grady's not firing me or anyone else. He's trying to take a vacation and wouldn't want to be bothered," I turned away and sat in a booth facing the checkout counter. The bells giggled on the front door, announcing the arrival of a new customer. I noted that Janeen completed her purchase without thanking the cashier. She turned, caught me watching her, flipped her thick ponytail, and marched out of the deli. Sighing to myself, I acknowledged I'd made a poor impression on my future colleague.

No worries, I thought, *that sassy superstar is way out of my league, anyway.*

CHAPTER 13
CONVERSATION
SKYLER

Four Days Later

At the end of the week, I was surprised to meet Janeen in the Back Country Deli a second time. Struck again by her beauty, I approached.

"Hi," I greeted. "What brings you back into the boonies?"

"Oh, yay. You again," she sighed.

"I hang out here for the free coffee refills."

"The coffee here is wretched," she sniped. "I prefer the café in town."

"Since I haven't run into you at the academy, I thought you split for the rest of the summer. Why are you still here?"

"Looking for a place to rent," she kept it brief.

"You signed your contract?" I inquired with a hopeful heart.

"No, I'm still considering my options. Why do you care?"

"I care about our girls, who need strong role models on staff," I clarified. "If Grady believes in you, I want you on our team. May I make a suggestion about your living arrangements?" After a brief pause, she nodded once sharply to invite my advice. "Why don't you live on campus for a term? Take your time to check out the scene."

"What scene?" she snorted, then complained. "There are only two Podunk villages within commuting distance of the academy. How can you stand it?"

"If you like antiques, quaint coffee shops, and musty bookstores, perhaps you'll appreciate the unique character of the towns," I challenged.

"Forgotten, forlorn towns from yesteryear. I've seen the same signs at every dingy bar and greasy diner. Knights of Columbus, Moose Lodge, and Elks Lodge. 'All You Can Eat Friday Night Fish Fry,'" she offered a scathing review of the small but friendly communities near the academy. "What do you do, anyway?"

"You've got a lot of nerve! I'm kinda into privacy," I teased.

"Did anyone ever tell you, you're not funny?"

"I'm the residence director."

"You're the residence director at a girls' school? But you're a *man*."

"In the halls themselves, all the advisors are young women. Recent college grads," I set the record straight.

"I can't believe in the middle of fricking nowhere you supervise a team of twenty-something females. That's highly inappropriate. A woman should occupy your position."

"My assistant director is a woman."

"Good for you," Janeen snarked. I expected her to walk away, but she didn't. "How did you end up working at the academy?"

"Well, the short version is that I rose through the ranks from desk key to assistant director during college. In the summers, I directed camps for high school girls on campus. After graduation, I applied to the academy. Since I had experience in co-ed dorms, Grady hired me," I smiled. "And now, four years later, you find me here."

"Why would Grady want someone with co-ed experience?" Janeen looked suspicious.

"You'll have to ask him."

"I fully intend to when I tell him how inappropriate it is for a man to be the residence director at an all-girls school."

"On campus, miles from the nearest town, a man can come in *handsy* sometimes," I teased again.

"You don't look like much of a man," she muttered.

"Sorry, what did you say?"

"I said; I heard your double entendre. I'm not going to play sexist word games with you."

"I didn't mean to imply anything sexual," I was taken aback. "I job-share with my assistant director, who I already told you is a woman. Nearly everything I can do, she can do. Admittedly, she prefers to leave some of the dirtiest jobs to me."

"You're pathetic," she mistook my rationale for another pun. "Fortunately, we won't be working together."

"Why is that?"

"First, I find your position of authority over female employees offensive. Second, your quote, girls in the boarding school need strong *female* role models—" she stopped short.

"Strong female role models like you?" I suggested.

"Yes, I'm a perfect example for the girls," she snapped. "But I'm being considered for a coaching and training position. Nothing more. I stay in the gym. I keep to myself," she drew sharp lines around her little world.

"These girls don't enroll themselves, you know. Their stinking rich parents *send them away* to boarding school," I hoped she could relate to the students the same way I had come to see them. "Our girls are not college co-eds eager to keep their scholarships who can be shuffled off like adults at a university. These are middle- and high-school-aged girls; they need trusted adults to go to in every situation. If one of your volleyball girls gets into trouble, who do you think will handle it?"

"Trouble?" Janeen perked up. "What kind of trouble?"

"Last year, for example, a group of mean girls posted lies on social media. It led to a catfight complete with hair-pulling and slapping," I explained.

"Mean girls?"

"Yes, gangs of them seem to find each other," I sighed. "Physical brawls are rare; they prefer shunning, ditching, and body-shaming. The academy counselor says these kinds of conflicts are normal given the isolated environment with no boys around—"

"That's totally chauvinistic," Janeen interrupted.

"Our counselor is a woman. Her words, not mine."

"Well, *you're* ignorant nonetheless. And I don't allow that kind of behavior on my teams," Janeen shook her head with haughty self-assurance.

"I'm sure you don't. All the same, if one of your team members is involved in a similar situation, you'll be called on to help."

"That's not in my job description," she flipped her ponytail.

"In the fall term, we always have runaways," I outlined another challenge she could expect to face in her position at the academy. "At one time or another, every kid gets homesick. These girls need a kind shoulder—"

"Nope. Not my job," Janeen didn't let me finish.

"Grady probably didn't talk about these unwritten rules in your interview," I wanted to caution her, having witnessed how well my boss could 'sell' the academy when he was on the scent of a coveted new hire. "Our girls are teenagers far from home. Many are international. Their biggest struggle during the long winters is loneliness. Most experience anxiety and depression." Apparently, I touched a nerve because Janeen's reaction was swift.

"You think you understand girls?" she sneered. "You don't know anything about the complex emotional life of a girl! Please, don't flatter yourself. A man, or a boy in your case, can't begin to understand the needs of a teenage girl. Don't bother me with your pop psychology," she flipped that ponytail again. What did it mean? I was intrigued by Janeen's mind as much as I was enamored with her perfect body.

"I'm no expert, I suppose, but growing up, I was close to a girl," I said.

"I'm not interested in your sex life."

"Sorry, I should say, a girl lived down the road from my house when I was a teenager. Her name was Chelsea; she was a close friend. I learned a lot from her," I tried to explain.

"Chelsea, huh? I bet you learned a lot. I feel sorry for her, poor girl."

"I've worked with schoolgirls for years," I felt called to defend my credentials. "Four years in residential life and four years on the job at the academy—"

"I guess that explains why you're weird," Janeen interrupted and checked her phone for the time. "Frankly, I don't care about your résumé or you. I'm not babysitting any teenage girls. I'm not a counselor, either. I'm a volleyball coach and an elite athletic trainer. I'm supposed to toughen up your girls and turn your pathetic sports program around. I win championships. There's no time for sentimental small talk on the road to a championship."

"I have a proposition for you," I hoped to chip away the layer of ice around my goddess's heart. She looked shocked. "Come out to the academy. I'll give you a tour. It'll be fun."

"No, thanks," she held her hand in my face. "I'm not interested in spending any more time with you. You're rude, boring, and misogynistic. Besides, I'm on vacation."

"Boring, perhaps," I allowed, "but I take offense at being called misogynistic."

"Early impressions are most revealing," she said whimsically. "You ought to work on that. Run along, now. Goodbye," she marched away without a backward glance.

CHAPTER 14
INTRUSION
JANEEN

August

I cruised into the town nearest the academy to begin the next chapter of my professional life. A mile past the Back Country Deli, I turned and parked in a gravel lot. A faded sign over the awning on the barn-like building read *Country Mart General Store, Bar & Café*. Every conversation stopped when I walked in. The patrons resumed their private talks only after the owner nodded at me.

At the café counter, I ordered a black iced coffee and then settled in a window booth. My future boss, Grady, bounced in and sat across from me just as the barista delivered my drink. Grady smiled hugely, practically vibrating with excited energy, and laid a thick manila folder on the tabletop between us.

After we signed my employment contract in triplicate, he said, "I'd love to stay and pick your brains about revitalizing our training program, but I'm headed out on vacation with the family. Guess it'll have to wait till term starts." He started to bounce out the door but turned back and said, "I almost forgot to tell you. The first fall staff meeting is in my office bright and early the day before classes commence. Don't miss it!" He waved and departed.

I gazed out the window and daydreamed. Signing the contract felt right, but minor worries still chased their tails in my head. Minutes passed. Skyler entered the café. With a sigh, I hunched down and away from the door. Unfortunately, I'd been spotted.

"Hey, Janeen," without asking permission, he moseyed over and took Grady's recently vacated spot. "What brings you to the best little café in town?"

"This is the *only* café in town," I pointed out. "It's a good thing you're not teaching etiquette at the academy. Do you always sit next to strangers without asking permission?"

"You may be a tad exotic, but I wouldn't say you were strange," Skyler smirked. *Someone needs to teach manners to this moron,* I decided.

"For your information, the word 'exotic' has profoundly dark and perverse sexual undertones. Animals are exotic, not women."

"I said exotic, not erotic," he joked. I stared at him, keeping my face expressionless. "It was meant as a compliment. You're different from most women I know," he shrugged.

"Watch your words," I warned. "My olive complexion *is* strange in this rural white backwater. And *you're* strange to me."

"Are we really strangers?" he sat back and mused aloud. "We're colleagues, aren't we?"

"I suppose we are," I admitted begrudgingly. "You just missed Grady. We finalized my contract."

"Congratulations," Skyler's face lit up. "May I buy you a cup of coffee to celebrate?"

"I don't let men pay my way, so don't ever ask me again. It's a paternalistic and condescending practice."

"I'm sorry."

"I *don't* accept your apology," I turned away and pretended he wasn't there.

"I wasn't apologizing *to* you. I was merely saying, I'm sorry you misunderstood me and took offense." My mouth fell open, and I debated whether to march out the door to teach him a lesson. He cleared his throat and said, "Look, Janeen, I want to be a good colleague and ally. I realize we may have gotten off on the wrong foot or maybe both wrong feet. May we start over?" I pointedly stared out the front window into the deserted street. "Hello, Janeen, may I please join you?" he persisted. Conscious that I was coming off as a royal bitch, I softened.

"Yes, you may," I gave him the once-over. He was smallish for a man, with long brown hair and a pretty face. Not intimidating as far as men went. I sighed and explained, "Quitting a secure job and starting something new has me a bit unnerved. I've been off for weeks."

"No worries," he looked relieved. "What enticed you to leave your college gig and join us at the academy?" I'd been practicing how to respond to this inevitable question.

"The short version is that the college administration wanted to expand my job description. I didn't want the new assignments. I ran into Grady, and he made me an offer I couldn't refuse." *There,* I thought, *that struck the right balance between openness, privacy, and profes-sionalism.*

"I am truly sorry we got off to a bad start," Skyler apolo-gized again. "I'm positive you'll make a fine addition to our staff. If you have questions, you're always welcome to ask me."

"Thanks," I wanted friends in this lonely new setting, but I wasn't sure I wanted a friend in this peculiar man-child. Or any man. I didn't count many men among my friend group. None, in fact.

"Did you find a place to live?" asked Skyler.

"Yeah. Maybe you know it? It's a single-story dilapidated motel on the edge of town. Converted into cheap long-term studio apartments."

"Skyler, your order's up," called the barista. She was stuck at the counter serving a growing line of customers.

"Back in a sec," he excused himself. I watched him surreptitiously. Apparently, there was a problem with his order. While he waited his turn to get a freshly made cup, I ditched the booth. We'd been intimate enough for one morning, in my opinion. After browsing the general store side of the building for a few minutes, I approached the cashier to ask a question. I noticed Skyler looking around for me. I pressed my lips together and advanced to the register. Skyler rushed over.

"Do you mind?" I snapped. "I need to buy some personal products." I waited until he took a few steps back, then whispered to the girl at the cash register, "I looked all over this hole-in-the-wall for feminine products. I don't see any on the shelves."

"I saw you talking to Grady and Skyler. You must be the new coach at the academy," said the clerk, full volume. "We keep a few boxes behind the counter along with the condoms. If we put the condoms on display, the local boys steal them. If we set out the tampons, the local girls steal them," she laughed. "What do you need? I recommend these," she showed me a box. "My periods are ghastly, though. Maybe you need something more like these," she waved a different box under my nose. I wished she'd shut up about it and let me choose without all the commentary. "Stock is low due to tourist season. What size do you want?" she held one box on each palm, moving them up and down as if weighing them against each other on scales.

"Just give me the regular-sized tampons," I whispered.

"Did you say jumbo pads?"

"No," I felt my face turn maroon. "The pink box. Not the jumbo ones!" She held it out. I snatched it and about-faced to continue shopping. Skyler stood in my path with his coffee in hand. "Men," I barked. "You're all disgusting. Are you satisfied? You invaded my private space, and now you know the size of my tampons!"

"If I knew you needed feminine products, I could've given them to you for free—"

"Don't you know when to shut up?" I cried in anguish.

"I keep a closet full of tampons and pads," he paused. "Well, I don't keep them. I pay for them from the academy budget. I order them, and the resident advisors maintain the stock for the students and themselves. I implemented the program because I believe that access to feminine products is a human right." I glared at him, trying to telegraph my deep embarrassment. "Well, you can ask my assistant director if you need more," he grinned.

"Just stop," I begged. "I thought you understood; I like my privacy."

"Not much privacy at the academy," Skyler remarked. "When do you start?"

"September, of course, like everyone else," I avoided his eyes.

"I'm not like everyone else—"

"That's for sure!"

"—I run summer school, music programs, and camps in the summer months. Our residence halls are open year-round. I'm on call 24 hours a day, seven days a week, fifty-one weeks a year. I get five days of paid vacation annually." It sounded like pure drudgery, and he actually seemed proud of it.

"Pardon my French, but what the hell? Are you an indentured servant? Ever hear of the Emancipation Proclamation?"

"I enjoy my job. I'm twenty-seven and one of the nation's youngest resident directors," he bragged. I said nothing. "Other resident directors envy me."

"Don't you have a personal life?"

"Work *is* my life. It's my calling and my Christian service," he kept explaining as the baffled look on my face intensified. "I just wanted you to know that not everyone at the academy works nine to five, Monday through Friday."

"Okay," I drawled as if I were negotiating a hostage situation with a raving lunatic. "Here's my advice, Skyler the overworked. This summer, perhaps you need to reconsider your priorities. You know, I gotta go. See you at the start of term."

"Why don't you ride out to the campus with me? I can show you around the residence halls and introduce you to some of the staff," he repeated the offer he'd made the last time we met.

"You must be kidding," I couldn't believe the moron was hitting on me. "First, I don't ride in cars with strange men. In fact, not with any men. Second, I wouldn't get in a car with *you* in a million years. Third, I'm sailing with my sister this afternoon."

"You're welcome anytime to be my guest at the campus," he persisted. It never ended. I was sick of hapless, aggravating Neanderthals who hit on me without being invited. I turned and walked away. "I can arrange a meal for you in the dining hall. Pot roast dinner tonight, delicious," Skyler called after me.

"Sounds disgusting," I called back without turning around. "I'm outta here. Remember, unlike *you,* I have the whole summer off, and *my* summer is filled with plans!"

CHAPTER 15
CONTRACT
GRADY

A Week Later

A calendar notification popped up on my screen, alerting me that Skyler was due to arrive at my office. I shook my head fondly. Skyler was my favorite protégé, but lately, he'd been giving off a strange vibe. I decided it'd be good for him to cool his heels for a while before I let him in. I picked up the phone to call an old fraternity buddy.

"Yo, what up, bro," I greeted. "I just pulled the biggest coup d'état in the business. You'll never guess what it was."

Clint, who oversaw the staff of an elite college just across the state line to the south, guessed, "You got a million-dollar donation for a new athletic field."

"No, man. Way better than that. I snagged Janeen. You know, the shit-hot college volleyball coach."

"No way! Why would she ever want to work for you?"

"I won her over with my charm."

"She *is* shit-hot," Clint gratified me with his awe. "And she's supposedly a total prima donna. What'd you promise her?"

"Besides a shag anytime she wants one?"

"You wish," Clint laughed heartily.

"As I said, my good looks and effervescent character made it an irresistible opportunity. Besides, you know the athletic director she's been working for. He's a chump. Remember him from the Panhellenic National Conference?"

"Whatever, man. How'd you do it, honestly?"

"You gotta feed the ego when dealing with high-caliber athletes," I revealed one of my trade secrets. "I told her I followed her career through high school and college. Promised that if she worked for me, she could write her own ticket. Blah, blah, blah."

Clint snickered, "And they call your pet residence director Skyler a wheeler-dealer. He's a slick negotiator, but you've mastered the art of the deal."

"I taught that kid everything he knows," I laughed. "I'm training him to be my successor."

"You been holding out on me, Grade? Got your eye on a new position somewhere?"

"I'll never tell."

"Rumor has it that since your appointment to Executive Director, contributions are soaring, and the Board loves you."

"Just doing my job, building on the foundation established by my predecessors," I humbly declined the compliments, even though they were music to my ears. "I'll probably stay here until I retire."

"Dude, Grady, you're the man."

"Thanks, bro," I'd had enough stroking. "Hey, speaking of Skyler, he's here for some schooling. Gotta bounce."

"Catch you soon, my brother. And let me know when those offers come rolling in so I can apply for your rejects."

"Sure thing," I hung up and opened my office door. Skyler was pacing in the lobby of the administration building. I waved him over. When he joined me, I pointed at the straight-backed chairs along my office window and waited for him to sit. I reclined in the giant leather chair behind my desk and eyed my heir apparent. Relishing the moment, I flashed my biggest smile and rubbed my hands together.

"I have news for you," I announced. "You may be a so-called wheeler-dealer, but I've outdone you this time. I landed us a world-class volleyball coach."

Skyler nodded matter-of-factly and said, "While you were on vacation, I heard the rumors. Then I bumped into Janeen at the deli on the highway." *What the hell,* I wondered. *The kid's getting too big for his britches.*

"Skyler, you have no idea how huge this is," I glowered, leaning forward over my heavy oak desk. "Let me explain what's going down. Did you know Janeen's high school volleyball team won two state titles? Two! From day one, as a freshman in college, she started on varsity. All four years, she led her team to nationals."

"Impressive," he looked unimpressed.

"Think of the parents who'll rush to enroll their girls here just because she's our coach," I leaned back and tented my fingertips under my chin. "I can't believe she'll be working for me. It's what this school needs to really set apart our athletic program."

"How long have you known her?" asked Skyler, finally cottoning on to the subject du jour.

"The athletic director at her college is a friend of mine.

A few years back, when Janeen was captain, he gave me tickets to the finals. After they won, I made a point to congratulate all the girls. That was when I planted the seed with Janeen," I hoped Skyler appreciated how much time and effort it took to cultivate an astounding recruit.

"I heard that after graduation, she stayed and worked for the college."

"She did. My buddy appointed her as the assistant coach. A year later, the head coach resigned, and Janeen stepped up."

"Very inspiring," said Skyler unconvincingly. It seemed timely to remind him that he wasn't the only successful young adult in our sphere.

"You know, she's a few years younger than you. I think she's only twenty-four." Skyler had the good grace to blush.

"How did you get her to accept your offer?" he asked.

"Let me tell you, I stole her," I was thrilled to enlighten him.

"You stole her from your friend, the athletic director. Is that how you treat your friends?" It was said lightly, but I sensed tension beneath the teasing.

"Very funny, Skyler."

"Why would Janeen leave a prestigious college program to work at the academy?"

"I bumped into her last month running the harbor trail in town. We joined up and chatted. She said she was visiting a friend. A girlfriend," I paused. "I think she's a lesbian."

"You never miss a beat, do you, Grady?" I narrowed my eyes, unsure if he meant it as a compliment. Skyler was a quick study, but sometimes he didn't value the relationship-building aspects of running a successful school.

"Right," I chose to ignore the comment. "As Janeen and

I talked, it dawned on me that she doesn't want to coach college students. She wants to work with younger kids. I thought to myself, we're the opportunity she's been waiting for. And, of course, it serves our objectives, too. Enrollment is king!"

"You live and breathe this academy," noted Skyler.

"My boy, so do you. The academy is everything."

"I suppose I'm becoming a lot like you," he looked surprised.

"Watch and learn from the master. Watch and learn. Anyway," I continued, "I struck on one of my usual brilliant ideas. I sold Janeen on my stupendous vision. I told her she could start a strength training program for all our girls in every sport. Be the athletic trainer and head volleyball coach, and launch a new middle school volleyball program to build future championships," I beamed, recalling my conversation with Janeen.

"I gather she bought your idea?"

"I haven't lost my touch with the young women, you know, Skyler," I winked at him. "She was champing at the bit by the time we returned to the trailhead. I thought she would pee her panties! Last week, we met at the Country Café to discuss terms. Before her coffee was cold, she signed the contract."

"Grady, I believe you'd sell your mother," Skyler shook his head.

"For the academy, you bet I'd sell my mother."

"I heard you wrote Janeen a sweet contact. Teacher's schedule. No summers. I suppose you gave her two weeks at Christmas and a week for Spring Break, too?"

Ah ha, I thought. *Finally, we get to the meat of the matter. Little Skyler is feeling slighted. He plays a vital role at the academy but is ultimately replaceable. Janeen's different. Janeen's an asset! This is a lesson he needs to learn.*

"Janeen was getting those terms at the college. I had to match their offer," I justified innocently.

"How much are you paying her?" Skyler asked. It was my turn to be surprised. He wouldn't have dared pose such a sensitive question a year ago.

"Come now, Skyler. You know I can't tell you that. Must I remind you that academy employment contracts are private?" He looked suitably chagrined. "I'm willing to tell you this. The Trustees granted me the authority to make an exemption to the salary scale for exemplary talent."

"I'd like better terms in my contract."

"You're already set in stone for the upcoming school year. Perhaps in a year, we can talk."

"A year from now, we'll be in the middle of my next contract. You'll say you can't change anything again."

"My investment in your education is paying off," I complimented him to avoid an argument. "You're becoming a smart businessman. We'll talk next year."

"I'd like your commitment to discuss my next contract in January," he pressed.

"Sure, son, whatever you say, but don't you see? You'll benefit from my deal with Janeen. Our reputation will soar." Skyler didn't speak. "Mark my words," I continued. "This young lady is going to land our academy on the map. Since word of our Olympic-caliber prize catch leaked, our enrollment inquiries have increased by a third."

"Olympic caliber?"

"I already told you, my boy, Janeen was nationally ranked in high school and college. Last year, she nearly landed a position on the USA Olympic Volleyball Team. Where've you been the last few years?"

"Working for you," he deadpanned.

"I love your sense of humor," I laughed. "Didn't you believe me when I said Janeen is world-class?"

"From what I saw when I met her over the summer, she's a world-class snob," Skyler said. I wondered if we would have a personnel conflict on our hands.

"Let me share a story to bring back your perpetual smile," I soothed. "Yesterday, the guys in town at the coffee roundtable called me Big Skyler. That's a compliment to you! They said you're Little Skyler, the little wheeler and dealer on supplies for the residence hall. I'm Big Skyler, the wheeler and dealer in the lives of everyone at the academy. I'm Mr. Academy. I'm growing the program so that, some-day, the school will survive without me in the hands of my successor. Stick around for ten or fifteen years. By then, you may be ready to take my place," I maintained a light, playful tone despite my message to Skyler that he was not in charge. Not yet. "I have to hop on a teleconference, son. We'll talk again after the staff meeting."

Skyler stood up and let himself out of my office without a word.

CHAPTER 16
DECISION
JANEEN

The Next Day

nxiety hit hard about a week after signing my contract. Sitting in the valley between two mountains of half-unpacked boxes in my cruddy roadside studio, I called my sister Colette.

"Hey, you," she answered on the first ring.

"Hey, boo, how are you?"

"Busy, boo-boo. You know, the summer drill. Group classes in the morning and lessons till quitting time," as a tennis pro at a private club, she coached players of all ages and skill levels. "What's up?"

"I need to talk."

"I've got five minutes. Give me the highlights," she put on her big-sister hat.

"Last week, I met with the academy director and signed my contract. Everything's been moving forward but...last night, I felt a twinge of buyer's remorse," I downplayed the depth of my second-guessing.

"Congrats! Why the remorse?"

"Several reasons. One problem is the location. The academy is in a godforsaken part of the state," I sighed.

"Um, last time I checked, that 'godforsaken place' is surrounded by an amazing national forest. Get outside, go hiking, enjoy the great outdoors."

"The place is isolated, Cole! It's way out in the sticks."

"Lest you forget, my dear sister, in college, you stayed on campus like twenty-four-seven. You barely went home once a month," she reminded me. "What's the difference between a remote town and a big city when you don't even go anywhere?"

"Okay, but this place is Never Never Land. To reach any sign of civilization, you have to drive for miles. When you finally get somewhere, you emerge from the forest at a dumpy little shack called the Back Country Deli," I made a gagging sound.

"When did you lose your sense of adventure, Miss Olympic Hopeful?"

"Sissy, I met my new boss in the nearest hick town. It was like a scene from a National Lampoon movie. He's a big-talking, self-congratulatory, hyper-masculine type. I can deal with that; there's certainly been plenty of those in my life," I snorted. "But the town itself? Ugh. A lonely cross-roads with a few antique shops open only during the summer tourist season. I could barely choke down what passes for coffee at the Country Mart General Store, Bar & Café!"

"Aw, the widdle biddy baby didn't get her bottle made wight," Colette teased. "You're butt-hurt because they didn't have your special dark roast imported brew, huh?

What'd you expect?" Her tone shifted. "I know you, little sister. Exactly what is bugging you?"

"I don't know if I made the right decision. Should I spend the rest of the summer looking for a position in the Twin Cities or Madison? What about Chicago?"

"Go ahead. What would it hurt? If you find something interesting, you're in a commanding position to negotiate. Treat the academy like a fallback," Colette encouraged.

"I don't know. I'm so conflicted!"

"I have an idea. Remember Megan, who used to go club-hopping with the tennis team? She was in the year between us."

"Yeah," I remembered Megan vaguely as adorable, outgoing, and a little ditzy. "Why?"

"I told one of my tennis moms that the academy recruited you. Turns out, Megan nannied for this woman's boss during college summers. Megan works at the academy! She's a talker. Reach out. She'll give you the down and dirty."

"And you were going to tell me this exactly when?" I demanded. "I would have liked to talk to her before I signed the contract!"

"Cool your jets, little sis. I just had this conversation a couple of days ago. Besides, the last time we talked, you were salivating over this job. How would I know you'd want to talk to her?"

"Yeah, yeah. You're right, as usual. Thanks for the pep talk, big sis."

"You're welcome, Neen," she said. "My next student's here. I gotta run. Love you, boo!"

"Love you, boo-boo," I grinned, ended the call, and hopped on social to find Megan's info. Her profile said she was the academy's curriculum director. I dialed. Megan picked up after a couple of rings. We chatted briefly, renewing our acquaintance. She was enthusiastic to hear about my contract, and we agreed to connect the next day at the Country Mart Café.

"Hello, Megan," I approached her from behind, where she sat in the booth I'd recently shared with Grady. I reached out to shake her hand. "Thanks for agreeing to meet," I tried to sound bubbly, but my stomach was full of butterflies. Worse than before the national finals. Worse even than before my Olympic tryout.

"Oh, it's my pleasure, Janeen," Megan smiled, emerald eyes sparkling as she looked me over. "I heard the rumors that you were joining the academy. I'm excited they're true! Finally, another woman my age to chillax with when we're not grinding away."

"Yeah, about that," I hesitated to burst her bubble. "As I told you last night, I signed the contract. But before I step into my position, I have a few concerns I want to be addressed. I was hoping I could talk to you, off the record, about the academy's work environment."

"Absolutely, you can trust me," she nodded, setting her red curls bouncing around her shoulders. "It's totally understandable that you have questions. The academy is a unique workplace," her brilliant smile re-ignited. "So, shoot. What are your concerns?" The barista approached to drop off my coffee, giving me a moment to gather my courage before I began.

"Throughout school, all the way up from elementary, I was on a volleyball team. After graduation, I coached my former college teammates. It was a dream job; I had the freedom to pursue my Olympic training and trials and continue my education, plus it kept my name in the national conversation about a sport that's as big a part of my life as breathing. Frankly, I'm stunned and finding it difficult to believe I left the college."

"Huge change. Just huge," Megan's eyes shone with compassion.

"I'm trying to wrap my head around it all," we sipped our coffees in silence for a moment. Finally, I asked, "What can you tell me about Grady, the academy's executive director?"

"Grady's a straight shooter. What you see is what you get," she shrugged. I wanted more specific details.

"What's his attitude toward females?"

"Girls or women?" Megan chortled.

"Start with the students, the girls," I was going to have to get used to the vocabulary all these academy employees used. Girls meant students. Women meant the adults responsible for the girls.

"Grady has two teenage girls of his own. He respects our students. He's a big advocate and wants equal opportunities for girls." I was pleased to hear his gender bias wasn't as exaggerated as I'd suspected. At least not when it came to the students.

"What about the women? His employees?"

Megan sipped her coffee, then said, "Although Grady's fair, he's old-fashioned. Somewhat chauvinistic. Can be condescending to women. It seems like he's trying to change. He's starting to give women more professional responsibilities." It all sounded very diplomatic. "He's old school with his male employees, too. At times, he goes into Air Force mode, barking commands. When he says jump, he expects men *and* women to ask how high."

"I'm okay with authority. As a lifelong athlete, I learned

to respect coaches. Some can be hard asses," I shrugged. "Grady was eager to hire me. He was generous with time off and benefits and gave me an amazing starting salary."

"If Grady likes an employee, then everything is good," Megan nodded. The longer we talked, the more comfortable I felt with her.

"Grady thinks I accepted his offer because I'm enthusiastic about the academy and its girls. That's not entirely true. May I tell you the real reason I accepted? Confidentially, of course."

"Your secret is safe with me," Megan leaned in.

"Thank you. Since I was working toward my master's degree in health and physical education, the college required me to teach an undergraduate course. Get this, they assigned me sex education! In the catalog, the courses were listed as Reproductive Health: The Body & Our Culture," I told her. "But everyone just called them sex ed."

"Reproductive health is so important," Megan said seriously. "Our girls would benefit from an updated and expanded sex ed curriculum. If you want to teach the course, you can do that. I'm sure Grady would be open to your suggestion."

"No way," I almost shouted. She totally misunderstood! "My college position *depended* on my teaching those courses. That's the *real* reason I wanted a new job. Pardon my French, but there was no fucking way I was going to teach sex ed."

"What's wrong with sex ed?"

"First off, it was *co-educational*. I'm only twenty-four years old! How old are you?"

"Twenty-five," Megan looked puzzled.

"I'm not about to teach nineteen and twenty-year-old boys, or girls for that matter, about sex."

"Sounds like a buffet," she licked her lips ostentatiously.

"Too embarrassing," I insisted. "Listen to some of the topics on the syllabus. Male reproductive organs, female reproductive organs, menstruation," my voice intensified. "Intercourse! Contraception! Pregnancy! Childbirth! Even freaking sexual abuse, Megan. Not to mention sexually transmitted infections and AIDS," I whispered the last bit.

"Sex is the most important subject on any college campus," deep dimples punctured her rosy cheeks, accentuating her teasing tone.

"Stop it. The course even included an LGBTQ unit, Megan!"

"Oh, yeah, essential," Megan batted her eyelashes. I sat back and decided to be totally forthcoming.

"You know, I always assumed I was heterosexual. Lately, I'm not so sure. While I'm feeling insecure about my sexuality, I don't want to teach the subject."

"This is timely," Megan turned serious again. "Last term, some girls wanted to discuss LGBTQ issues. They asked to form an extracurricular group. Grady was supportive but didn't approve the request. He's afraid the school board will object. His solution is to codify it as a course for next year. You know, take it through the proper channels. Like I said, he's old school. Maybe you'll be ready to teach it by next year?"

"Listen to me! I said no effing way. I'm the least qualified person to teach the course under any circumstances, anyway. No experience," I shrugged. "Senior year of high school, I had sex once. That's it. Dry spell before and a dry spell since. I'm a misfit." Megan's mouth fell open.

"But you're stunningly beautiful! For sure, guys ask you out."

"For sure, a bunch of mouth-breathing Neanderthals,

thinking with their dicks," I sneered. "Besides, I was completely devoted to my team. No time for guys or their penises."

Megan giggled, checked her phone, and asked, "Do you have time for another cup?"

"Sure. I'm going to my sister's later today. No rush," I watched her sashay to the counter and order for us both. A sneaking suspicion dawned in my mind. *Was she sashaying for me?* The building was deserted other than a grandmotherly-looking woman shopping in the store and us. Megan turned and smiled brilliantly when she caught me staring at her hourglass figure.

"Any more questions about academy life?" she settled into her seat and straightened her V-neck, so it perfectly framed her considerable décolletage. Again, I wondered if she was flirting with me.

"No, this has been very helpful. I appreciate your candor and your discretion."

"Okay, my turn," she smiled devilishly. "What was it *really* like to be a gorgeous volleyball star with a mega-hot body on a co-ed campus? I miss men our age," she sighed. "Especially when they're only thinking with their penises."

"For crying out loud, what do you think it was like? I'm a female athlete. You've seen our volleyball shorts, haven't you? All my life, boys stared at me. They came to the matches to drool at our asses," I unintentionally rhymed. Megan choked on her coffee, trying not to laugh. "Look, I can deal with guys and how they undress me with their eyes and all their Neanderthal bullshit," I shuddered. "Even teaching them, I could have dealt with all of it. The girls were the final straw when it came to quitting my job."

"Uh, you realize you signed a contract to work at an all-girls academy, right?" Megan looked worried.

"How could I teach girls about their bodies? I ran five miles a day. I hit the gym for hours afterward. Plus, volleyball practice. For several months each year, my periods stopped. Pardon my French again, but my menstrual cycle is fucked. I'm not in any position to teach other girls about their reproductive systems," I wanted her to understand where I was coming from.

"I'm going to sell your story. Listen to my byline," Megan cleared her throat, straightened up, and the devilish grin reappeared. "'All-American Collegiate Athlete, Afraid of Sex, Quits Her Team! Story at eleven.'" It did sound funny when she said it that way.

"You better not say one word, you promised," I smiled.

"Your secret is safe with me," she crossed her heart and held up two fingers. We finished our coffee over the less intense topics of the weather and how we'd spent our summer vacations.

CHAPTER 17
SUBMISSION
SKYLER

September

"Let's get rolling on the new academic year," Grady called our pre-term administrative staff meeting to order. He radiated pride in his hand-picked squad, who circled to find their places around his big conference table. "I'm pumped, folks! I trust you're rested from your long vacations." I resisted the temptation to correct him. I'd barely enjoyed a week off. Everyone settled and came to attention.

"Let's begin with staff announcements," he practically bounced in his seat; he was so excited. "Welcome to the newest team member I bagged, Janeen!" Applause erupted. "Everyone, introduce yourselves. We'll go around the horn, starting with the big man on campus. Don, you're up." Glancing at the assembled party, I realized no one besides me was surprised by Janeen's presence.

"Excuse me, Grady," I cut in. You could've heard a pin

drop. "I thought this was the *administrative* team meeting. Wasn't Janeen hired as a coach and a trainer?"

"Skyler, my boy," though Grady spoke lightly, I could tell he was annoyed at my interruption. "Do I need your permission to make decisions around here? Let's step outside the office for a moment." I didn't budge. "Go on, do as I say," Grady ordered quietly. Reluctantly, I stood, walked around the remaining seated staff members, and out the office door, which Grady left wide open. "Turn around," he commanded. Conscious that everyone could see and hear us, I obeyed. "Read the sign above my door. Tell us, what does it say?" I looked at the sign but didn't reply. "We can't hear you, son. Speak up," said Grady loudly.

"Executive Director."

"As long as Executive Director is written over my door, you'll follow my instructions. Thank you, you may return to your seat," he followed me back inside, then addressed my colleagues and me. "I may consult you on certain matters when I think your expertise is valuable. However, I never need your advice or permission before I make decisions. Agreed?" Grady pointed around our little circle.

"Yes, Grady," said everyone in unison. Everyone, that is, except for me. When I heard them submit to his ego show, I thought, *it's time. There's no dignity in this! I need to find a new position.*

As if to prove my unspoken point, Grady called me out again, saying, "Am I losing my hearing? I don't think I heard Skyler. What did you say, my boy?"

I cleared my throat and said, "Yes, Executive Director." I almost saluted him but held back, choosing not to further test his patience.

"That's more like it," he crowed, good humor restored.

"To answer your question, last week, I appointed Janeen to the position of Interim Athletic Director. That's why she's here."

"Thanks for telling me," I didn't try to cover up my sarcasm.

"Aw, Skyler, feeling left out?" Grady stared me down. "I informed the team last week while we were preparing for the term. Where were you? Oh, that's right. You were off traveling around the country. You would've known if you didn't take your vacation just before the start of the school year. In fact, if Janeen chooses to accept, I plan to make her appointment permanent," he concluded magnanimously, looking over at Janeen to gauge her reaction.

"I took a vacation at the end of August because my contract requires me to work every day of June, July, and most of August. I'm on-call 24 hours a day," I felt I must defend my absence to my colleagues.

"No need to be argumentative, my boy. I was just stating the facts. Now, that's settled. Go ahead, Don; please proceed before Skyler derails us again."

"Hi," Don cleared his throat and waved awkwardly in Janeen's direction. "Like he said, I'm Don, Facilities Director."

"Don't be shy, Donny," Grady jumped in. "Tell us how long you've been at the academy, and share one of your goals for this year."

"Ah, let's see. I've worked for Grady for ten years. I aim to oversee the completion of the new band and orchestra practice rooms by winter break."

"Come now, Don! Why do I have to drag it out of you? Tell Janeen about the new volleyball practice facility," urged Grady.

"Yes, that's right," Don blushed. "Over the summer, the

Board approved a big new project. We're seeking bids for two indoor volleyball courts and a covered outdoor sand pit. Construction should begin late winter, and the facilities should be completed before the start of the next season," he looked at Grady to see whether he was satisfied.

"Thanks, Don, my main man. Great update."

"Welcome, Janeen," piped up the middle-aged woman beside Don. "I'm Amber, the academy's principal. Seven years' tenure. If one of your girls struggles academically during the term, I'll keep you posted. I'd like us to sit down after the staff meeting. I want to review the team's class loads with you."

"Sounds great. I look forward to working with you," said Janeen eagerly.

"Your turn Megan," called Grady.

"Hey, Janeen, hello again," Megan waved exaggeratedly at Janeen, who sat beside her. "Janeen and I are already acquainted. You could say we have a mutual friend. I don't need to introduce myself."

"Megan, follow the directions," sighed Grady.

"Okay, fine," she smiled broadly. "I'm Megan, Curriculum Director. Two years at the academy. Janeen, I look forward to working with you, too. Teachers submit their lesson plans to me each Thursday for the following week. I'd appreciate it if you could stick to the timeline for your weightlifting classes."

"That's unnecessary, Megan," Grady looked like the cat who swallowed the canary. "As Athletic Director, Janeen will report directly to me." Megan looked skeptical but kept her mouth shut.

"Your turn, Skyler," Grady turned to me.

I nodded slightly at Janeen and said, "Janeen and I met earlier this summer."

"Oh, you did, did you? Follow the routine, Skyler, my boy," insisted Grady.

Self-conscious in the extreme, I complied, saying succinctly, "Skyler. Residence Hall Director. Starting my fifth academic year."

"Skyler's too modest," Grady took over when it was clear I wouldn't elaborate. "He's doing a fantastic job! Under his leadership, morale and extracurricular activities participation are at all-time highs. And Skyler restored parental confidence in residential services by holding semi-annual parent days when caregivers may join us for an overnighter to experience academy living. Skyler, please give Janeen a tour of the residence halls soon." He leaned confidentially toward Janeen and added in a stage whisper, "While Skyler may complain that he works all summer, he enjoys a few nice perks, too. The academy covers his room and board. He lives in the historic limestone cottage overlooking the lake. Skyler, be sure to show Ms. Janeen your quaint home," Grady raised his eyebrows at me.

Pride still smarting, I reminded my boss, "Are you forgetting your rules, Grady? I'm not allowed to have a woman in my cottage."

"A tour, Skyler. Not a sleepover! A tour during broad daylight is acceptable. Megan can chaperone you and Janeen if you're uncomfortable." A smattering of apprehensive chuckles erupted.

"I'd love to see your place," piped up Janeen. "Whenever you're free, Skyler, please let me know." I didn't respond. After a pause, Grady spoke again.

"Let me close this agenda item with my personal welcome, Janeen. We've got great expectations of you. I'm confident our athletic program and the volleyball team will be awesome this year. If you need anything from me, drop by my office anytime."

"Thank you, Grady. Everyone's been so kind. Megan and Skyler have been most helpful," acknowledged Janeen. She and Megan exchanged a bright smile, then she looked at me. I stared straight ahead.

"Moving right along," Grady cleared his throat and looked down at his paper agenda. "Each fall, I reiterate the academy's work schedule policy so everyone's on the same page. Administrative staff workdays are Monday through Friday, plus three Saturdays monthly. As for Sundays, I will not command anyone to labor on the Lord's Day," Grady looked at me. "Of course, these rules don't apply to Skyler. Residential life carries on seven days a week. Any questions thus far?" he scanned our faces. The room was silent. "Married staff are required to work one night a week. Their unmarried counterparts work four nights a week."

"Excuse me, Grady," I raised my hand, breaking his rhythm. "May I ask a question?"

Looking mildly irritated, Grady called on me, "Go ahead, Skyler."

"Can you explain why unmarried employees work four nights a week while married employees work only one?" I watched the mild irritation flare to full-blown impatience.

"That's always been our policy," he stated matter-of-factly.

"Are you willing to explain the rationale?"

"Why are you asking, Skyler? The policy doesn't apply to you. You're our twenty-four-seven-three-sixty-fiver," he deflected.

Megan raised her hand and spoke without being recognized by Grady, "Skyler has a few hours free, doesn't he? For example, if I want Skyler to run out with me for coffee on a Saturday morning, may he?" Everyone stared at Megan. Grady looked shocked for a split second, then regained his composure.

"Of course, Skyler may take a few hours off on the weekend," he laughed uncomfortably. "Only now and then, mind you! You kids go ahead. Have some fun. I'm not an ogre."

"Grady, with all due respect, I'd like to know the rationale for the policy on married versus unmarried staff," I repeated.

"No one else is asking for reasons, Skyler," Grady said. "However, since you insist, I'll explain. Married staff members are typically older and more experienced. They've earned the right to more time off and extra time to spend with their spouses and children. Unmarried staff members do not share the same family responsibilities. Now, onto our next—"

"Grady, I beg your pardon," I raised my hand again. "I have a follow-up."

"Skyler, can we please move along? I answered your question." I felt the tension mounting in the room.

"If I get married, what happens to my work schedule?" I asked. Janeen giggled, then covered her mouth with her hand. Likewise, Megan struggled to contain her amusement.

"What did you say?" Grady guffawed. *"You?* Get married?" Everyone in the room shifted awkwardly in their seats. Well aware that one of Grady's favorite pastimes was trying to embarrass me, I pressed on, undaunted.

"If a single man works five days and four nights a week and on weekends, when does he have time to find a girlfriend and get married?" I asked with a straight face. As if I'd pressed a release valve, my fellow team members burst out laughing. Even somber old Donald couldn't resist. Though Grady typically possessed a great sense of humor, my challenge to his authority was too much.

"Are you interested in girls, Skyler? I assumed you batted for the other team."

Everyone stopped laughing, and Janeen said accusingly, "Grady, that's not funny."

"Oops," Grady paused long enough to take the room's temperature. "Did I say something politically incorrect? Sorry, I come from a different generation. We made jokes about queers," no one reacted. "There I go again; I mean the gays and lesbians. If there are any homosexuals on staff, I didn't intend to make fun of you. At least not to your face," he laughed nervously when he realized no one was willing to participate with him in his swinish attitude. "Sorry, folks, I suppose that's none of my business. Not too many years ago, you know, we had a policy against hiring homosexuals. If we discovered one, we fired them. No questions asked. You understand why, right?" he trailed off. No one spoke. Clearing his throat, he turned the conversation back to my question. "Skyler, here at the academy, we're family. Married employees are parents. Their children need extra consideration. We're all helping to raise their kids. What's the saying? It takes a village!"

"The policy is unfair," I said. "What about divorced staff members? Or unmarried ones with kids? Or even married ones without kids?"

"No one's ever challenged this policy, Skyler, and this is neither the time nor place to start. Raise the matter with me outside a staff meeting if you must persist."

"When are you free to meet? I'd like it to be sooner than later, as I can no longer accept a workplace policy that discriminates against unmarried staff."

"Skyler, that's enough," Grady's face turned bright pink. "I will not tolerate insubordination! If you don't like the academy's policies, you can quit. There are plenty of people willing to take your place."

"Grady, I simply asked for a meeting time—"

He cut me off, saying, "Our policies regarding married and unmarried staff were in place long before you began working here. They were laid out in every contract you signed. I expect you to comply as you agreed to, as you have in every past year. Will you be doing that, Skyler?" I didn't answer. Inside, I boiled. "Skyler, you will abide by the policies. Won't you," he wasn't asking. No one breathed or moved a millimeter. I considered standing up and walking out of the room, but I knew there'd be consequences. I wasn't prepared to face them just yet.

I quietly said, "I've always followed your rules."

"Good. I expect you to set a better example. Enough about this," Grady closed the discussion.

As the meeting continued, I silently plotted my resignation. Though I cherished my position and was willing to work hard to achieve my goals, I finally realized how overloaded and exhausted I'd become. The academy's policies were only a small component of my dissatisfaction. Grady had subtly demeaned me in front of my colleagues for as long as he had employed me, but this was the most blatant instance.

When I finally refocused on what was being said, I heard Grady announce, "The final item on the agenda is new business. After a decade of controversy and discussion, the Board has decided we are going co-ed." Everyone except Janeen applauded. Grady continued, "Our long history as an all-girls academy is drawing to a close. We'll be opening a boys' dormitory next fall. During his college years, Skyler worked at a co-educational campus, so he'll be leading the charge. Congratulations, my boy! I'm confident you're up to the task and will execute our integration brilliantly." This was the first I'd heard of my new assignment, but I knew I could handle it. The only question was, did I want to?

"Thank you, Grady," I said graciously. "I look forward to the challenge. I'm confident I'll succeed with the cooperation of everyone in this room." All of my colleagues nodded, except for Janeen again! I wondered why she looked alarmed, but it wasn't the time to ask. A round of applause broke out. Grady dismissed the meeting, and we all went our separate ways.

CHAPTER 18
PERKS
JANEEN

October

Surprisingly, as the school year wore on, I found I liked working at the academy. My new volleyball squads gelled nicely, and my training program produced quick results. The students, or 'the girls' as everyone else referred to them, were generally eager to participate in my PE classes. Every week, my relief was renewed that I was not being forced to teach sex ed curriculum. Jarred as I was by Grady's announcement of the Board's plan to integrate boys into the school, I didn't fixate on it. I decided that when the time came, I would insist on teaching and coaching girls exclusively. Until then, I focused on my duties.

Since Grady had been so generous with my time off, I could leave campus most weekends unless I had volleyball responsibilities. I chose to spend most of those weekends with my sister. Megan and I grew closer as the weeks passed. Although our personalities were vastly different, we enjoyed each other's company. Before long, we fell to spending every Thursday evening together, eating pizza or burgers at a greasy bar in one of the local towns.

On a Thursday night in mid-October, during one of our girls' nights out, I asked, "What's Skyler's deal, anyway? I've barely interacted with him; he's über-busy with planning for the new boys' dorm."

"He's wound up tight. We're talking snare drum," Megan did a rimshot with her fingers on the edge of the laminated wood table. "Wants the academy to be a *professional* place of employment. Follows all the rules. I guess I'd call him anal-retentive." We laughed.

"How do you get along with him?"

"I like working with Skyler. He tries to get along with me," she looked thoughtful. "I think perhaps I'm a little too bohemian for his tastes. Too unstructured."

"I mean personally. What's he like?"

"Oh, personally," she quirked a manicured eyebrow. "Let's see. Skyler lives to work. He fully embodies his director role. When I catch him with his guard down, which is rare, he's still rather reserved. Always polite and kind, mind you! I gather he's afraid to be himself," she sipped her beer and studied my face. "Why do you ask?"

"I ran into him a few times last summer. When I did, he insisted on talking to me. Of course, like all men, I felt him undressing me with his eyes," I blushed and was thankful for the dingy bar lighting. "That's why I'm surprised, as you said, to find him so enthusiastic about embodying his professional role."

"Ooh, scandalous," Megan pursed her lips. "I've never seen that side of him. Honestly, he strikes me as very respectful of women." After a pause, she added, "Strangely, he's somewhat like you."

Shocked at the comparison, I exclaimed, "No way, Megs! We're not talking about the same guy. Skyler and I are polar opposites."

"I beg to differ," Megan rebutted. "Like you, he's totally committed to his work. His staff is his team. He lives to serve them and make them great. You've gotten to know Holly, Kiva, and a few other resident advisors. Have you heard them say one bad word about Skyler? No way! They're loyal like troops. Not out of fear. He does everything he can to make their jobs easier. He may not join in the fun, but he gives them space to blow off steam. He keeps a courteous, professional distance. But he's always there like a trusty cousin." As she detailed them, I could see the parallels between Skyler and me. She may have been describing my approach to managing a volleyball club.

"I met him at the deli on the highway twice," I said, twirling my beer mug in a pool of its own sweat. "We had coffee together once. He came across as serious about his work, but he was painfully socially awkward. Looking back, I think he was afraid of me. Kept tripping over his words."

"Promise not to tell anyone if I tell you a secret?" Megan flashed her dimples. "I like Skyler. I mean, I *like*-like Skyler. Don't you think he's adorable, with that luscious long hair and pretty face? I could be the fire to his straight-laced ice. We'd make a perfect couple."

"He's a skinny kid, not my type," I crinkled my nose.

She continued, "I only wish he'd loosen up. I wish he'd ask me out. But then, Skyler doesn't go out. He's always working. Maybe I should invite him on a campus date," her eyes went unfocused, looking past me. "It'd be so romantic. I could cook dinner for him in his cute little cottage by the lake. Then, we could walk in the woodlot behind his place, and I would take his hand in mine. We'd sit in the grass and kiss," she trailed off dreamily.

"You're lovesick," I shook my head and laughed.

"No, I'm starving for affection in this lonely place," said Megan sadly.

"Have you told Skyler that you like him?" I was more interested in her answer than I cared to admit.

"What's the point? If he can't see that I like him, there's not much hope," sighed Megan. "And he's not allowed to have a girl in his cottage, which ruins the fantasy."

THE NEXT DAY, I OBSERVED SKYLER IN THE DINING hall at lunch. I recalled Megan's lovestruck rumination and had to admit he was cute in an androgynous way. As I watched him make his rounds, pausing to interact with several students and his team members, my thoughts wandered to his motivations. What made him tick? He was so serious! All business. I wondered how he managed to be so utterly devoted to his work. Didn't he long for meaningful relationships with people his age? Why hadn't he gravitated to Megan or me as a friend outside work hours? We were co-directors, and none of us reported to each other.

Skyler looked up as he moved from one table to another and caught my eyes on him. He smiled briefly but continued about his business. Not what I expected of a man who was so eager for my attention just a few months ago.

At that moment, I decided to enlist Megan to make Skyler our project for the balance of the year. Maybe our united efforts would lighten this kid up!

CHAPTER 19
MISCHIEF
JANEEN

October

On our next girls' night out, Megan and I hung out in her dorm apartment after work hours. We ate mini taquitos, watched TV, and talked. I revealed my hopes for our joint humanitarian project to bring Skyler out of his shell. Excited and ready for mischief, we decided to drag him out of his cottage without delay. We slipped on our shoes and walked across the chilly grounds.

Outside Skyler's place, we hid under the hemlock trees that ringed his property; we mustered our courage, leaped out, and pounded on his front door. At first, no one answered. We kept pounding.

"We know you're in there, Skyler," Megan pressed her lips against the door crack and shouted. "Don't be shy. Let us in!" Finally, we heard footsteps on the wooden plank floors. An interior door opened and closed.

I sang in a young girl's falsetto, "Can Skyler come out to

play?" Megan laughed raucously. I continued, "Two drop-dead gorgeous girls are waiting on your front porch to take you out!"

"Did someone get hurt? Is a student missing or sick?" Skyler answered the door in his bathrobe, looking concerned.

"Skyler, you have a problem, and this is an intervention," I announced. "All you do is work, work, work! You need to get a life. Megan and I are taking you out."

"I can't leave campus," he looked dejected.

"We knew you'd say that," Megan and I said in unison, sharing an exaggerated eye roll.

"Get dressed. You need a little excitement in your life, and we're here to provide it. Let's go," I insisted. "We won't take no for an answer."

"Where are we going?" he asked.

"It's a surprise," I said. He started to look a little excited but also a little worried. "It'll be fun, I promise."

"Wait here. I'll get dressed," he retreated, leaving the door cracked. I peeked in and watched him disappear down a hall. When I heard a door close, presumably to his bedroom, I signaled Megan. We tiptoed into the living room. When Skyler reemerged fully dressed, he stopped short. Megan lay on the area rug, stomach down with her bum in the air. I was stretched full-length on the couch. Posing like two Playboy models, we laughed at his shocked expression. "You can't be in my cottage," he said fearfully. "Seriously, I can't be alone with a girl in my place. I'll get fired, and you'll get in trouble!"

"You're not alone with a girl, Skyler. Can't you count?" I teased. "There are *two* girls here. Actually, we're *women*. Which of us do you prefer, Megan or me?" Skyler paled and didn't answer. "Doesn't Megan have a nice butt?" I insinuated. "Look at it, sticking up in the air." Megan played along, waggling her pert derrière. Skyler's face turned pink. He shifted his slight weight from one foot to the other.

"Janeen, you're embarrassing him," Megan looked at me with a shadow of alarm. I ignored her.

"Shall we scream, Megs? Will security rescue us?" I wanted Skyler to react! He finally did.

"You wouldn't dare," he whispered. "Please leave."

"It's just a joke, Skyler," Megan rose to her knees. I pointed at her to be silent.

"We'll leave on one condition," I negotiated from my pose on the couch. "You're coming with us." Looking relieved but still uneasy, Skyler nodded, and I sat up. Megan and I grabbed one of Skyler's hands and pulled him between us once we were outside. Our newly formed trio trudged toward the dining hall. Upon sneaking into the kitchen, Megan and I made a beeline to raid the refrigerator.

"We shouldn't be in here," cautioned Skyler.

"Rules were meant to be broken," I intoned. Skyler stood stock-still, like a deer caught in headlights. "Don't worry. *You* won't get in trouble. If Grady finds out, *I'll* take all the blame. I have him wrapped around my little finger," I bragged, hiking my hip and lightly slapping my butt cheek. "He can't take his eyes off me. Have you noticed?"

"It's not like we're stealing anything, Skyler," Megan reassured him. "Look at it from this perspective. We get free meals with our contracts. You've heard of self-service?" she giggled. "Janeen and I creep in here all the time."

"Milk and cookies are my favorite," I held up a waxed paper carton and a tiny bag of Chips Ahoy.

"Don't forget the ice cream," Megan pointed at the industrial freezer.

"Skyler, stop," I commanded when he approached the wall. "Don't turn on the lights. Use your phone. Look, yogurt cups. Skyler, I found a flavor for you. Cherry!" Megan and I howled with amusement.

"You're so bad, Neen," Megan rested her head on my shoulder and gazed into my face. "How did I ever survive this place without you?"

"I think we should leave," said Skyler.

"Megs, we're freaking him out," I sighed. "I know; let's take our food to the staff cabin. There's a pizza over there in the freezer. We're gonna party!" Megan and I whooped and hollered.

"Not so loud," squeaked Skyler.

"We're just getting started, buddy," I slapped him on the back and pushed him toward the walk-in refrigerator. "Turn right and look behind the cases. I hide my beer in the back."

"No. Please, no beer on campus," moaned Skyler. "The staff lounge is closed for the night, too."

"Stop being such a goody-two-shoes," I said. "That's a ridiculous rule. It's barely after ten o'clock. We aren't the students. We're supposed to be adults. We work here, but we're not slaves. We have every right to party!" I let out a wild yahoo.

"Janeen, it's quiet hours. Please," Skyler begged. "Students are in bed."

"Skyler, my boy," Megan parroted Grady's voice and poked him playfully in the ribs. "You need to get a life. Stick with Janeen and me. We'll show you a good time." We loaded up our ill-gotten snacks, and each grabbed one of

Skyler's elbows. We practically dragged him to the staff cabin.

"It's locked," he looked relieved after he tested the door. "I happen to know it's dead-bolted," he started to back away.

"Not to worry," beamed Megan, pulling something out of her cleavage. "I have a key."

"Where did you get that?" Skyler paled in the moonlight.

"You forget Skyler, we're girls. We can get anything we want around here," Megan and I exchanged a knowing look.

Skyler said, "But how exactly—"

I interrupted, "Last week, we paid Donald a visit. We sweet-talked good ol' Donald," I paused. "No, let me rephrase. Megan *flirted* with good ol' Donny—"

"I'm not a flirt!" Megan proclaimed.

"Oh, my bad. I guess you flashed your gorgeous smile and batted your bright green eyes. Oh, and you wiggled in your short shorts. Maybe that's not quite the definition of flirting...but the result was the same! Donald gave you a key."

"I did not flirt with ol' Donny. Ew! He's married," squealed Megan, reaching to unlock the door. "I can't help it if I'm sweet, and he treats me like an incredibly adorable daughter." The door swung open to reveal the dark cabin interior. The three of us stepped inside.

"Stop it, Skyler," I had to remind him again. "Don't touch the lights. Let your eyes adjust. There's plenty of moonlight. Megan, turn on the oven. Let's get this party rolling!"

"It's late, and I need to be up early. You should party without me," Skyler said meekly.

"Aw, do something daring for a change. Stay with us," Megan whined.

"I have a long day tomorrow; I need to sleep," he turned as if to leave. I grabbed him by the shoulders and ushered him across the room.

"You're not going anywhere," I plopped on the couch. "Sit down," I patted the cushion beside me. Skyler settled as far away from me as he could. "If you're tired, you can rest your head on my lap. I'll be your pillow," I invited. "Or maybe you'd rather put your head on Megan's lap?" I tested. He didn't speak. "Come here, Megan, and sit on the couch with us," I commanded.

"Do you mind if I sit between you?" Megan sank into the middle cushion. I put my arm around her and squeezed her close to my side.

"Isn't she amazing, Skyler?" I said. Megan giggled. Skyler stared straight ahead. Irked at his unresponsiveness, I hopped up and spun around to face the sofa. I straddled Megan and sat on her lap. She looked slightly surprised but played along, wrapping her arms around my torso. I ran my hands into her wavy, fiery locks and bounced on her suggestively. Gazing into her eyes, I declared, "Skyler, I think I'm in love with this pretty girl." Skyler sat stiff as a board, motionless except for a jaw muscle that I saw twitching in the moonlight. I released my captive with a subtle laugh and stood. I headed to the kitchen and stuck the frozen pizza in the oven before returning to my spot on the couch.

While the pizza was cooking, Megan and I ate snacks and chatted. We teased Skyler about breaking the rules and staying up past his bedtime. Mostly, we teased him about being alone in the dark with two hot and horny girls. He did not partake in the banter. Although I couldn't see his expression clearly, I could tell he was totally out of his element. That was okay by me; I was accustomed to being on the receiving end of too much attention from the opposite sex. It felt good to turn the tables for once.

"Tell us, Skyler," I quizzed. "Did you date girls in high school? Did you have a girlfriend in college? Were you ever engaged?"

"No."

"No, what? No dating? No college girlfriend? No, you were never engaged?" Megan pressured.

"In my senior year of high school, I liked a girl. We were just friends. We're still friends," Skyler said softly. "Her name is Chelsea."

"Since you moved here, have you dated anyone?" I asked.

"I don't have time for dating. I'm responsible for the food, lodging, health, and safety of all the students and my staff. I'm focused on my work."

"Yada-yada-yada," I yawned. "You're a broken record, Skyler."

"You can't give your heart and soul to your work. Or the students. Or Grady. The academy is Grady's legacy, not yours," Megan lectured kindly. "No one appreciates your sacrifices. If it's the last thing we ever do, Janeen and I will liberate you from bondage."

"Megan," I said sharply. "What if he likes bondage? Maybe we should tie him up. We could have our way with him. A little S & M. What do you think?" I sensed Skyler sliding farther away from us on the couch.

Megan grinned devilishly in the semi-darkness and embraced me. She kissed my cheek. I kissed her on the lips. For a split second, I slid my tongue inside her mouth. She gasped, laughed wickedly, and slid her hand onto my crotch. I buried my face in her hair and gazed over her head at Skyler.

"Skyler, if you're not going to play with us, Megan and I will be forced to gratify ourselves without you," I taunted.

"Then I'd better give you some privacy," Skyler said seriously.

"Aw! Stay, Skyler," Megan invited sweetly. "Stay and watch. You may learn a thing or two," she nuzzled my neck.

"I'm leaving now," Skyler stood up and started toward the door. The oven timer beeped.

"Pizza's ready," I announced and shrugged Megan off. "Don't go, Skyler," he paused but didn't turn around. "Megan and I know each other. We want to get to know you, too," I said kindly.

"Looks like you know each other intimately. Too intimately for colleagues," Skyler said sternly, finally about-facing.

"Listen to yourself," Megan jumped up and touched Skyler's arm. "You sound like an old man. We were only trying to have fun with you," she pleaded and looked at me to request backup. I could tell she was worried that Skyler might report us. "Janeen and I are not into bondage," she explained. "We're not lesbians either."

"Speak for yourself, Megan. How do you think I got elected captain of my volleyball team?" I continued to play with Skyler and Megan, confident in my control of the situation.

Megan looked at Skyler's face and pleaded, "Seriously, Skyler. We want you to come out of your shell. It's not healthy to suppress your feelings all the time." Skyler's shoulders slumped, and I smelled blood in the water. We'd won. I stood and grabbed one of each of their hands.

"Let's go," I ordered. "March. Pizza party!" Our trio

moved to the kitchen table. I served slices of cheesy pie on flimsy paper plates. The conversation turned to safe and familiar topics. While Skyler wasn't a big talker, he thawed as we lightly gossiped about the troublemakers at the academy and Grady's rough military exterior and warm paternalistic compassion for his staff.

Talk turned to our plans for Thanksgiving and Christmas. Megan was going home to her parents. I was going to my sister's. Sadly, Skyler was spending all his holidays on the academy campus. He didn't mention his family. I sensed he was estranged from them. Well past midnight, our party broke up.

After Megan and I deposited Skyler at his front door, we walked arm-in-arm back to my car, which was still parked near the administration building. Megan ambled in the direction of the dorm after a friendly goodnight hug. Driving back to town, I silently recounted the evening. Skyler seemed to enjoy being included in our girls' night out. I could see that Megan was not only crushing on him; she understood him at a profound level. I also noticed that Skyler respected and trusted Megan but liked her only as a friend.

A sly smile stole over my face, illuminated by the blink of the turn signal in the dark; I'd definitely found the answer I was seeking. I knew the power I held over Skyler. The only question was, what would I do with it?

CHAPTER 20
RECONNECTING
CHELSEA

November

"What do you mean I can't stay at your place?" I yelled into the phone.

"Girls aren't allowed in my cottage, Chelsea. I'm sorry, it's not my rule. It's my employer's," Skyler sounded contrite, but I was seriously miffed.

"Don't call me a girl," I'd be damned if I was turning around without seeing him after an eight-hour drive. "I'm not a student at your school. I'm a woman and your best friend. I drove a whole day to see you. I'm exhausted. I'm staying with you."

"I'll get in trouble," he said meekly.

"How's that a problem? You *always* got in trouble seeing me." He was such a rule follower. Obviously, that hadn't changed.

"You're right," acknowledged Skyler. "But this is different. I work here."

"Do you want me to leave?" I demanded aggressively, remembering that sometimes Skyler took more than a gentle push to follow his heart. It was too bad he was still such a child, letting others dictate his life. I waited while he ruminated, thinking I'd have been better off staying in the city with my college friend. I had Thanksgiving week free from work and took a road trip. After a day of shopping with her, it dawned on me that I was only a few hours from Skyler. I texted him the news and asked if he wanted to see me. He said yes.

"I'm waiting," I reminded him.

"Don't leave, Chelsea. I miss you and want to see you," pleaded Skyler. "You can come to see the academy, and we can walk and talk like we used to."

"Where do you propose I sleep?" I asked sarcastically.

"I can get you a guest room in the girls' residence hall."

"No, absolutely not. I didn't drive this far to sleep in a dorm, Skyler. I'm staying with you, or I'm leaving. Your decision."

It took a minute, but he finally sighed, "I guess you can stay with me. We'll need to be discreet, though. Don't tell anyone you're sleeping at my place."

"Fine," I huffed. "Nothing like a warm welcome from a long-lost friend. According to the clerk at this roadside bodega, I'll be there in a half-hour."

"Park by the administration building, and I'll meet you in the lobby," said Skyler. "And I'm sorry, Chelsea. I truly can't wait to see you."

"Yeah, yeah. Me, too," I relented. "See you soon," I hung up. As I followed the signs pointing to the academy down a lonely two-lane highway, I decided if I continued feeling unwelcome, I'd split after catching up for a few minutes.

This was supposed to be a vacation, for fuck's sake! Not an emotionally frigid reunion tour.

Skyler and I reunited in the bland lobby of the academy's admin building in due time. I was relieved to find him warmer in person. Our conversation quickly regained its comfortable old rhythm, and we started the tour. We didn't get far before we bumped into the infamous Grady, who greeted me with fake, overdone good humor. I watched him give my body the once-over and resisted the urge to shudder. During our infrequent phone conversations over his first several years at the academy, Skyler had extolled Grady's virtues as a boss and mentor. However, the last time we spoke, I sensed that Skyler's admiration had cooled considerably. Grady always sounded like a pompous ass to me. I tuned into his demeanor and observed him, keeping a neutral smile plastered on my face.

"Is your friend staying for dinner?" Grady asked.

"Yes. We'll eat in the dining hall," Skyler answered. "I want Chelsea to get the full academy experience."

"Be sure to charge her for the meal," Grady reminded him curtly. He winked my way and explained, "We have a twenty-five-dollar guest fee."

"Seriously, Grady?" Skyler said sharply. I was shocked at his tone. "I work here day and night. I haven't had a visitor in over a year. Are you honestly going to make me pay for her dinner?"

"Skyler, my boy," Grady reached out to pat Skyler's shoulder heavily. "There are no exceptions to the rule. If I let your guest eat for free, the next guest will want to eat for free. Before you know it, all the teachers, staff, and students will invite their friends to campus for a free meal. If you get your way, we go bankrupt," the buffoon exaggerated. I'd witnessed this behavior in plenty of older-generation men. It made me seethe, but I kept my cool for Skyler's sake.

"I am not charging my friend to eat in my dining hall," Skyler resisted. I silently cheered for him.

"I'll be checking with the cashier," threatened Grady.

"Fine," Skyler snapped. "I'll cover the cost."

"Enjoy your tour, Chelsea," Grady flashed me an oily smile. "I hope you enjoy your dinner, too. We have award-winning food services," he took a few steps and then whirled to face us again.

"Since Chelsea's from out-of-state, I assume she needs a place to stay? You know the rules about your cottage," he wagged a finger at Skyler. "I expect your guest will be staying in the girls' dormitory. Be sure to charge for lodging." I began to understand Skyler's hesitance to break the rules. This guy was a total power tripper.

"Nothing gets past you, does it, Grady?" Skyler rejoined. "You'd charge your mother for visiting the academy."

Grady guffawed as if it was the funniest joke ever, then said, "That's right, I would. No need to get touchy, Skyler. I'll give your friend a discount. Charge her a hundred for lodging. In fact, how about one-fifty for lodging, dinner, and breakfast? Sounds fair to me," accounted Grady. "I assume she's only staying one night. That's our guest policy, after all." Skyler gritted his teeth; I heard the enamel scraping.

"I'll have it deducted from my next paycheck," he said with forced calm. "Is that everything, Grady?"

"I think that should do it, my boy," Grady looked pleased with himself. "I'll poke my head into the accounting office and save you the trip. Have a good time."

Neither Skyler nor I talked for a few minutes after this encounter. I could tell he was fuming, so I let him have space. Hopefully, he saw how unhealthy this dynamic with his boss was; they were obviously on a collision course. Skyler regained his voice as we walked. He described some recent improvements to the kitchen and menu additions that rivaled the nation's best boarding schools. *He sounds like Grady Junior,* I thought. *They're definitely a toxic duo!*

The whole place bustled with pre-Thanksgiving break energy. Skyler and I entered the well-appointed dining hall, which was alive with students. We collected our food trays and sat at a table reserved for staff. Immediately, two of his colleagues joined us.

"Are you going to introduce us to your friend?" the redhead simpered.

"Megan, this is Chelsea. Janeen...Chelsea."

"Ah ha," exclaimed Megan. "The elusive Chelsea. We figured you were a figment of Skyler's imagination. The way he acts around us, we didn't think he'd ever met a girl before." Janeen and Megan laughed conspiratorially.

"Mystery is Skyler's modus operandi," I said. "Megan, Janeen, nice to meet you. Are you taking good care of him?"

"We try," Janeen leaned close. "If you ask me, we're too much for him. He avoids us when he can. We're the campus troublemakers," she and Megan chortled. "Was he always this serious?"

"Skyler's always been cautious and courteous with me. Get to know him; you won't find a more loyal friend," I complimented, smiling at Skyler.

"Tell us more," begged Megan. "Tell us a secret about Skyler."

"He's a good listener. He brought a ray of light into my dark life during a very dark time," I nodded seriously.

"Interesting," Janeen perked up. "Have you been

holding out on us, Skyler? I never knew you could *light up a girl's life,*" she insinuated, batting her inky lashes.

"It wasn't like that," stammered Skyler.

"Chelsea, were you girlfriend and boyfriend?" demanded Megan.

"You'll have to ask Skyler. I don't kiss and tell."

"Not to worry," Janeen asserted. "Since we found out you actually exist, we'll extract the truth from Skyler."

"Yes, during one of our late-night threesomes," Megan whispered. Skyler's face blazed bright red, and we three women laughed. He sat silently for the rest of the meal while we moved on to general get-to-know-you topics.

After dinner, Skyler and I walked around the campus and its grounds. We ended the tour at Skyler's cottage on the lakefront.

"Don't you want your own private room in the residence hall?" he asked hopefully.

"Are you kidding me?" I crossed my arms. "I'm staying with you. Especially after meeting that Grady character."

"What do you mean about Grady?"

"He's a chauvinistic douche, Skyler. Didn't you see him checking me out?"

"He doesn't mean any harm," Skyler defended. "He's old school, and he loves this place. With his military background, he's a stickler for the rules. He's not a tyrant or anything, he's just Grady."

"Yes, he is, too, a tyrant. I watched him with you. He's domineering, intimidating, and selfish. He's trying to humiliate you." Skyler looked self-conscious and dropped the protective vibe.

"Here's my dilemma," he unlocked the door to his cottage. "Being the academy's residence director is my dream job. On one hand, I love the work. On the other hand, the work is killing me."

"I'm proud of you, Skyler. Proud of your accomplishments," I told him as we entered the quaint little home. He turned on the lights after he locked the door behind us. "But can't you see that Grady is zapping the life out of you? He demands complete submission."

"Lately, I've been thinking it feels like I sold my soul to him," Skyler confessed. "And it's starting to feel like I sacrifice my body and mind every day to the academy. But I don't know where to go or what to do; I'm stuck at a crossroads."

"Well, I'm here for you. If you decide to leave, with or without another position, you can stay with me. I'll make room for you."

"Thank you, Chelsea," tears came to his eyes. "You are a true friend. I plan to make some big decisions about my future early next year. Your offer means the world to me."

While Skyler got ready for bed, I unrolled my sleeping bag on his sofa. We said goodnight when he came out of the bathroom, and he went to his room. I took my turn, brushing my teeth and staring in the mirror, thinking over the evening. Back in the family room, I reclined on the sofa and retrieved a book from my backpack. I tried to read for ten minutes, but thoughts of my friend and our history distracted me. I turned off the light and contemplated my feelings. With Skyler, I always felt accepted. I was glad I'd taken this rare opportunity to see him; it had been too many years.

A soft yellow light shone beneath Skyler's door. The desire to snuggle with him, as we did in my enchanted forest during our high school days, swept over me. I wanted to be close to my friend. Quietly, I tiptoed over the burnished wood floors and opened his bedroom door. He'd fallen asleep with his light on, a book lying open across his chest. At his bedside, I gently pulled back the blanket and top sheet. His eyes parted, and he smiled dreamily. I slid in next to him and wrapped one arm and one leg around his torso, nuzzling my head into his shoulder like I used to. He closed his eyes.

I broke the silence, "Remember, years ago, back in my woodlot, we cuddled under the magical white pines?"

"Yes. I loved being with you down in the dark ravine under the hemlock tree," he replied affectionately.

"Walking in the woods with you is the best memory of my life," I pressed my body into his. Skyler turned toward me, touched my cheek, and kissed me. My tongue found the inside of his mouth. I climbed on top of him, resting my breasts on his chest. He pulled down my pajama bottoms. He was excited. I was turned on. In a moment, he was inside me. I rode him hard until we climaxed together.

As if we were under our hemlock giant, I rested on Skyler for the longest time. Eventually, I rolled on my side. With our legs intertwined, we fell into a deep sleep.

CHAPTER 21
DIALOG
CHELSEA

Eight Hours Later

Thankfully, the next morning was not awkward. Skyler and I seemed to understand each other without talking about what happened. Despite Grady's plan to charge me for an overpriced award-winning dining hall spread, we hid out in the cottage, where Skyler made us a big breakfast. As we washed dishes afterward, he broached the subject.

"Chelsea, I'm glad you crawled into my bed. I enjoyed being intimate with you last night."

"Oh, sure. I liked sleeping with you, too," I agreed, wondering where this opening would lead.

"Why did you decide to do it?"

"Let's not ruin the moment," I sighed. "There's no need to overanalyze. I was horny. You were available," I saw the beginnings of an injured expression sneak onto his pretty face. "Don't get me wrong. It wasn't meaningless sex; we made love when we both needed it," I explained.

"You're a wonderful lover," Skyler said sincerely. I shook my head ever so slightly, realizing Skyler was still a boy, filled with romantic expectations for sex.

"Let's not critique the experience, okay?" I tried to find words that wouldn't hurt him or permanently alter our special connection. "Long ago, I knew I wanted to have sex with you. It couldn't happen in high school or college; I was too traumatized dealing with personal issues. During that era, I needed a friend. Not a lover. You were that friend. Moreover, we were near the same age, but you were too young, too much younger than me. Do you understand?" I could see him concentrating.

"You knew I liked you, right?" he finally asked.

"Of course," I reassured him. "That's part of why I came to see you again; to renew our friendship," I saw it dawn in his eyes. He assumed I was friend-zoning him. "Let me clarify. I want to remain friends. Best friends. But I'm not looking for a long-term romantic relationship right now. Not with anyone. We may have sex, or we may never have sex again. Either way is okay by me."

"Yes, I understand," he nodded slowly. "I'm contemplating leaving the academy. I applied for a few jobs back home. Eventually, I want to get my master's degree."

"That would be awesome, Skyler," he was beginning to see the situation as I did. "Here's my suggestion. Be sure you understand the reasons you want to leave this position. Don't let our interlude last night influence you. It's normal to reconsider career paths in the late twenties. It's a transitional time."

"It's scary. I have some big decisions ahead of me," he searched my face as if to ask my advice.

"You seem desperately alone here," I observed. "Not to be confused with lonely. Despite daily contact with dozens of people, you appear to be *alone*. Is there anything or anyone keeping you at the academy?"

"Yes," he admitted. "First, it's the security. This is the only workplace I've known as an adult after college. I'm familiar with academy life. Second is my loyalty to Grady. He's been my guide and my mentor. Grady trusts me. I feel like I owe him." Recognizing Skyler's struggle with his toxic dance partner, I sought words that wouldn't push him one way or the other but would give him food for thought as he looked for answers.

"At one time, Grady was instrumental in your life. Maybe he has big plans for you. It's hard to know what others are up to or whether we can rely on their promises. Be careful. He doesn't own you," I paused. "Let me ask, what about the girls? Are the girls keeping you here?"

"The students?" he misconstrued my meaning, but I didn't correct him. "I strive to make a positive difference in their lives," he said thoughtfully. "If I remain at the academy for my entire career, I'll develop lifelong relationships with a few of them. Years from now, some of them will remember me and return to visit. If I quit, I'll lose the connection with this school and the students forever." While this wouldn't be one of my reasons to stay in a thankless, soul-sucking job, I understood its appeal to Skyler.

"That's a powerful reason to continue with your position," I acknowledged. "But I wasn't thinking of the students. I meant, what about the young women on the staff? Specifically, the two I met last evening."

"Megan and Janeen?" Skyler looked puzzled.

I chided, "You may know something about your students, Skyler, but you can't read your colleagues."

"What about Megan and Janeen?"

"They like you," I said.

"Sure, we work well together. Grady's a great team builder. Sometimes, the three of us hang out after hours."

"Skyler, listen to me," I decided to enlighten him. "They like you. Catch my drift? They really, *really* like you. It's obvious that one or the other wants to be more than a friend."

"No, we're just friends," Skyler looked genuinely surprised.

"You're wrong," I said. "I'm right. I have a woman's intuition in this matter, and I'm an outside observer. As you entered the cafeteria, their faces lit up," he opened his mouth to argue, but I continued. "I saw it, Skyler! When they noticed me, their eyes gave them away. Megan and Janeen were jealous," I paused. "Grady owns you. Now Megan and Janeen own you, too."

Skyler shook his head in denial, "I don't believe you, Chelsea."

"Stay here long enough, and you'll discover the truth," I decided to let it go rather than risk an argument. "At any rate, if you choose to move on with your life and you need a place to lay your head, you're welcome to crash at my place," I reiterated my offer and left it at that.

CHAPTER 22
PERSUASION
SKYLER

December

D uring October and November, each Thursday after lights out, Megan and Janeen knocked on my cottage door. Janeen always had an action plan. She was our ringleader. Despite remaining on campus, every excursion was thrilling. We shot baskets in the cavernous gym with only the safety lights illuminating our games. We held hands and walked the lakeside trail in the chilly starlight. We jogged on the indoor track, racing and frolicking like kids. We always raided the industrial refrigerator in the dining hall kitchen. I truly enjoyed my time with the girls. I'd never experienced camaraderie as they offered it, and I'd never been part of the in-crowd. It felt good to be included at last.

Though my days were busier than ever with coordinating the expansion of the academy's campus to accommodate co-ed residence life, it was challenging and exciting, and I wouldn't have missed a minute for the world. Grady, while still regularly enforcing his will on me, eased up on the humiliating banter. Our working relationship went on smoothly enough. It was a golden time in my life.

Janeen invited Megan and me to her apartment on the first Thursday in December. I got permission from Grady to leave campus for a few hours without too much hassle. Janeen made burgers and French fries. She served a huge bowl of ice cream with three spoons for dessert. After dinner, we played board games. The girls chattered non-stop about the games and their favorite movies. They talked for an hour while I listened. Apparently, I was too quiet for Janeen's taste.

"Why are you so sullen, Skyler?" she asked.

"Am I that transparent?" I replied with a tight smile.

"Aren't you enjoying your time with your two hotties?" asked Megan.

"Being with you two is the best. I regret that we didn't do this last year," I looked back and forth between them.

"We couldn't, duh," said Megan playfully. "Janeen wasn't here. We needed her. Are you sure you're okay?"

"I'm just deep in thought," I told them.

"We're all friends here, Skyler. Open up and talk to us. We can tell something's on your mind," insisted Janeen. I hesitated a few seconds.

"I'm thinking about going to graduate school."

"That's exciting," exclaimed Megan. "Will you take summer courses?"

"I'm considering resigning from the academy. Quitting and going full-time for my master's." The girls fell silent, and the glow on their faces disappeared.

"We don't want you to leave," Megan spoke first. "You belong here. The three of us have a great time together."

"Are you sure about this?" Janeen looked skeptical. "Have you even applied?"

"No, I haven't applied," I said, feeling guilty for bursting our happy bubble. "I spend way too much time thinking about my job and not enough time planning for my career."

"You're good at your job. You love your work," it sounded like Megan was accusing me. "Why do you want to leave all of a sudden?"

"It isn't a new idea, Megan. I'm sorry it upsets you. Since you work here, I won't say anything disparaging about the academy. But I wanted to be honest with you when you asked what was on my mind."

"It's Grady, isn't it?" Janeen's dark eyes narrowed. "You don't want to work for Grady anymore."

"Grady's been good to me. I can't criticize him."

"Grady is tough on you. I see you interact," Janeen nodded. "But he's your friend, too. He likes you. He wants you to succeed," she watched me closely. "If it's not Grady, then what's your problem?"

"You two helped me see what I was missing. I want a job that doesn't consume me. A job that allows me to go out more often. I want a social life!"

"You *have* a social life with Janeen and me, Skyler," Megan practically shouted. "Stay! Don't make any hasty decisions."

"Is there something you're not telling us?" Janeen fished for more information. "What about your visitor? Thanksgiving week, you introduced us to Chelsea, the clever one with the curves."

"She's a friend," I said.

"Girlfriend?" Megan probed.

"She's a girl. She's a friend. We aren't boyfriend-girlfriend," my voice shook a little. Janeen and Megan exchanged glances. The room went eerily silent.

"Janeen and I are dying to know," Megan pressed. "You can be honest; your secrets are safe with us. Where did she spend the night?"

"Chelsea insisted on spending the night in my cottage," I confessed.

"You dirty dog," Janeen cried out. "Listen to him, Megs! He wouldn't give us a tour of his cottage a few weeks ago. Once we got him out of his shell, there's no stopping him," she laughed a hard laugh that didn't sound like her normal self. "Skyler, you never cease to amaze us. You're a fast learner," it didn't sound like a compliment.

"Skyler, you've got to stay at the academy," Megan insisted. "Can't you see the three of us together? Next year is going to be great."

Janeen seemed to shake something off and joined in, saying, "Megan and I will provide you with a full social life. Right, Megs?" Her partner in crime nodded enthusiastically. "You want to go out more often? No problem. We'll take care of you," she promised.

"I appreciate you both more than you know. I've never had friends like you. I'm in a quandary. But I need to make some big decisions early next year," I said somberly and checked my watch. "It's time for me to get back to campus. I don't want to antagonize Grady."

Our party broke up.

CHAPTER 23
PROPOSAL
SKYLER

Two Weeks Later

During the third week of December, teachers administered finals. Friday afternoon, parents started arriving to take their children home for the holidays. I stood in the residence hall lobby wishing everyone who walked past a Merry Christmas. Since many of our international students couldn't travel overseas for the break, my contract obligated me to remain at the academy and provide a modest schedule of activities. While I managed the chaos of luggage and departing girls, Janeen graciously supervised an optional open gym time for those who were staying. In the evening, the faculty and staff hosted a holiday feast for all that remained. Janeen, I noticed, was absent from dinner. As I oversaw the post-meal cleanup efforts, I was surprised to receive a text from her.

> **Janeen**
> I want to see you in my office before I leave.

After confirming that an advisor was on duty in the residence hall, I stepped outside. The moonless night air was bitterly cold. As I crossed the quadrangle, my boots squeaked on the crisp snow. Academic buildings that normally blazed brightly at all hours loomed dark and lonely. A single security light pierced the pitch black to guide my footsteps across the eerily silent grounds. Finally, in the darkness, I spotted a dull yellow glow emanating from the gym. I sped up. When I pulled on the main front door handle, I discovered it was locked. I tried the staff entrance. It, too, was locked. I could have opened the door with my master key, but I didn't want to startle Janeen.

> **Skyler**
> Outside the gym.
>
> You still here?

> **Janeen**
> Use your key.

I opened the door and walked to her office.

"Hi," I announced myself. "I'm surprised you're still here. What's up?"

"Come in, have a seat. The day after we return to campus, the basketball team has a game. I'm wrapping up a few details."

"Are you still driving to your sister's tonight?"

"Yeah, she's holding dinner for me."

I waited while Janeen worked, watching her. She wore a snug-fitting white ski parka, zipped partway up. A fuzzy white V-neck sweater left a triangle of olive skin exposed at her neck. The duo of snowy fabrics accentuated her thick hair, which spilled in a lush black waterfall over her shoulders. I quietly admired her wintry ensemble until she shut down her computer. When the fan stopped whirring, Janeen popped out of her chair to reveal the skintight black jeans she'd paired with her top half. She stretched luxuriously and sat on the credenza next to her desk.

"Skyler, I stayed at school this evening because I wanted to catch you before you make any ill-advised life decisions," my curiosity was ablaze, but I waited for her to finish. She appeared to debate with herself for a moment. "Are you still planning to speak with Grady in January?"

"Yes, that's my plan. Unless he's willing to rewrite the terms of my contract, I have no reason to stay another year. It's only fair to give him plenty of notice." A pause ensued.

I almost fell out of my chair when Janeen asked, "If I marry you, will you agree to continue working at the academy?"

"Wait, what? What are you talking about?" I stuttered, then regained a bit of composure. "You told me you didn't want to date anyone!"

"If you sign your contract and continue to live here, I'll marry you," she offered unromantically. My initial reaction was to shout, *yes! A thousand times, yes!* I would have married her in a heartbeat; to me, she was the most beautiful woman in the world. My heart wanted me to say yes, but I didn't.

"Janeen, I adore you. But you said I was your friend. You said you wanted to be best friends," I couldn't help wondering, *am I being set up? Is her office microphone on? Is Megan listening?* My thoughts spiraled to her motives. If I said yes, would Megan barge into the office and howl with laughter? If I said yes and signed my employment contract, would Janeen dump me? Scenarios rife with humiliation and devastating feelings unfolded in my astonished brain.

Amid these imagined sequences, I recalled a long-forgotten memory. As a young teenager, I was smitten by a girl. She told me she lost all her money at the fairground. I gave her my cash. Then, laughing and sneering, she opened her purse and showed me her wallet stuffed with dollar bills. She didn't steal my money. I let her deceive me. Was this another blind infatuation, and was I again playing the role of the fool?

"Well, now I'm offering to marry you if you meet my conditions," Janeen crossed her arms over her chest and blinked at me.

"I need time to think."

"That's fine. We can talk after the break. I need to get on the road to Colleen's," she checked her phone. I began to fear that my moment had passed.

"Can we meet in the main lodge in an hour and talk?"

"No, I'm running late," she said flatly.

"I can follow you to town, then. Let's stop at the Country Mart Café for a quick cup of coffee and talk," I pressed.

"No. I don't want your answer tonight, Skyler."

"You know I think the world of you, don't you, Janeen?" I didn't want her to leave until we settled this. "We should talk tonight. You asked a life-changing question; we need to talk."

"I have another condition," she held up a hand. "I will not speak with you again until you talk to Megan. She wants you to date you, you know. Frankly, she's in love with you. She wants to marry you, have your babies, and work at the academy forever. She's a lifer."

Baffled by this turn in the conversation, I said, "I suspected she liked me. But I had no idea she wanted to be my girlfriend."

"I'm talking lifelong partner, Skyler, not girlfriend-boyfriend," scoffed Janeen. "Look, before I speak with you again, you must clear the air with Megan. While I'm on break, take her out one night. Resolve these issues."

"Janeen, how would I even start that conversation?" I demanded. "Please, you and I need to—"

"Just do it! She's my best girlfriend. I can't marry you unless you set her straight," instructed my goddess. "After I return from my sister's place in January, we'll meet in your cottage," she eyed me critically. "Don't come to me. I'll come to you," she walked out of her office with a sharp nod and a familiar flip of her jet-black hair.

CHAPTER 24
REJECTION
MEGAN

Ten Days Later

After spending Christmas Day with my parents, I excitedly returned to the academy to help coordinate activities for the students trapped on campus for their winter break. I got to work side-by-side with Skyler for the entire week. While I missed the threesome we made with Janeen, I reveled in holding all of Skyler's attention for myself.

I about died of happiness when he asked me to spend New Year's Eve with him. I arrived at his cottage in the early evening for a dinner of snacks and sodas. We played board games while I daydreamed about being married and living in this charming little place as a couple. Later, we bundled up in our coats and boots to walk outside.

The sky was clear. The night air was crisp in my nostrils. We strolled arm-in-arm behind the cottage, where moonlight illuminated the meadow backing up the property. A familiar trail emerged, edged in silver. Upon reaching it, we switched to holding hands.

At first, we walked without speaking. The only sound was the creaking of our boots on the fresh snow. Soon I heard the wind passing through the white pines and hemlock trees in the nearby forest. I leaned my head on Skyler's shoulder.

"Skyler, I like working with you. I like spending time with you. I hope you're not leaving the academy," I spoke in a low voice. "If you stay, I'd like to be more than friends."

"Megan, you're one of the nicest people I've ever known," began the letdown. "I like you. I want to remain friends. If I misled you, I apologize."

"Don't apologize," I could tell he was feeling bad. "We never talked about our friendship or labeled it," I pulled my hand out of his and wrapped my arm around his waist. "Truthfully, I'm disappointed, but you didn't mislead me."

"I'm sorry to hurt your feelings," he said kindly, putting his arm around my shoulder.

"May I ask, are you attracted to someone else?" I hesitated, then stated my suspicions. "Are you in a relationship with Chelsea?"

"Chelsea's great, but she doesn't want a boyfriend. To be honest, I'm attracted to Janeen," he admitted.

"I had no idea," I gasped. "You never showed feelings for her!"

Skyler said, "Maybe you've noticed I'm afraid to talk about feelings." I chuckled sadly. He continued, "I didn't want to expose myself to the possibility of getting burned. It's happened before."

"You okay if we keep walking?"

"I'd love to," said Skyler. I guided us out of the meadow and down a pathway toward the woods.

"I can't compete with Janeen. She's spontaneous and beautiful. I understand your attraction to her; I love her, too," I confessed.

"Relationships aren't a competition," Skyler looked concerned. "You're a wonderful person."

"If you hadn't met Janeen, would you be interested in me?"

"I can't answer that. I met Janeen. The past is what it is."

"If you change your mind, I'll be waiting for you," I pledged.

"Please don't wait for me, Megan. I'm not good enough for you." Although Skyler claimed not to have much relationship experience, he certainly knew what to say to deflate a woman's ego!

"Let's keep walking. I want to savor this moment. It's so romantic under the hemlocks on a cold winter's night," I smiled to let him know I had no hard feelings. We strolled without speaking until my toes were frozen.

Upon returning to Skyler's cottage, we watched the Times Square Ball drop on television. We welcomed the new year with a platonic hug. Afterward, Skyler accompanied me to my car, which was parked at the administration building. Janeen and I had moved into a rental house in town together during the last week of the semester.

When we paused to say good night before he turned back to his cottage, I couldn't resist grabbing his coat collar and pulling him close. I kissed him softly on the cheek, then let go.

"Happy New Year, Skyler. May all your dreams come true," I whispered as I watched him walk away.

CHAPTER 25
SURRENDER
SKYLER

January

E very hour of every day of the break, I contemplated Janeen's proposal. On the first of January, I received a text.

Janeen
Happy New Year!

See you at 7 PM tomorrow, your cottage.

On the second of January, the academy was still closed. I spent the day alone, rehearsing what I'd say to her. As the grandfather clock struck four in the afternoon, I began pacing in the living room.

At five and again at six, my stomach churned. At six-thirty, I made a bowl of soup and a grilled cheese sandwich. I gagged on one small bite of the sandwich and dry heaved. I stopped trying to eat.

When the grandfather clock struck seven, my nerves were frayed. I checked out the front window every five minutes until the clock struck eight. Janeen never showed.

At nine, I texted.

> **Skyler**
> Are you OK?

> Are you still coming tonight?

The grandfather clock struck ten. No Janeen and no word. I was an anxious wreck. At eleven, I considered calling the Sheriff to report her missing.

At last, at eleven-thirty, someone tapped on the door. My heart thumped. I opened it. Wordlessly, Janeen stepped inside and stomped the snow off her tall black boots.

"I'm sorry I'm late," she said after a moment.

"No problem," I lied.

"I couldn't get away from Colleen's. She begged me to stay another night because of the heavy snow and terrible roads."

"I understand," I lied again. My feelings were knotted in a pretzel. My life, my entire future, depended on the outcome of our conversation. Yet, it didn't seem to matter to Janeen. After spending two weeks with her sister, I wondered why she hadn't left earlier to be with me. Why didn't she call? Was a simple text too much to ask?

"I only stopped to tell you I made it back. Let's talk tomorrow evening or later this week," she started to leave. I put a hand on her elbow.

"You're here now. Let's talk," I couldn't take any more suspense. "Come in, please. Have a seat."

"I'm tired of sitting. I've been sitting in the car forever."

"Can I make you a cup of tea?" I offered.

"No, I don't have time for tea."

"Here, let me hang your jacket," I moved to take it from her shoulders. She pushed her balled-up fists deep into the pockets.

"No, I'll wear it. I'm going soon." Perplexed, I let my hands drop and stared at her. She stood there, looking around. Pretty soon, she pulled her hands out and rubbed them together as if to warm them. "So, did you go on a date with Megan?"

"I talked with Megan. I wouldn't call it a date."

"Would *she* say it was a date?"

"She might, but not because I misled her," I clarified.

"What did you do with her?"

"We had snacks and played games here at the cottage, then went for a walk."

"Where to?"

"Down the meadow trail and into the hemlock grove—"

"You're kidding," she interrupted. "Into the woods? What time of day was it? Did anyone see you walking with her?"

"It was probably ten at night," I guessed. "No one saw us."

"Strolling with a lady after dark? Sounds like a hot date."

"It wasn't intended to be romantic."

"Did you walk with her on New Year's Eve?" Janeen eyed me suspiciously.

"Yes. What's the big deal?"

"You're so naïve," she moaned. "If you take a girl on a walk all alone at night on New Year's Eve, no matter what you tell her, she'll think she's on a date. It's the second-most romantic night of the year!"

"I told her it wasn't a date," I protested. "If she thought otherwise—"

"Did she touch you?" Janeen interrupted again, making my head spin.

"Let's see," I wanted to be honest, and I was wary of being caught in a miscommunication if Janeen cross-examined Megan the same way she was interrogating me. "We walked arm-in-arm the way the three of us always do until we got to the meadow. Then, we held hands and walked under the hemlock trees on the new snow."

"So, you walked with Megan on a cold winter's night, all alone through the meadow, into the forest, holding hands," jealousy gilded her tone.

"Nothing happened," I started to sweat. "I only did what you told me to."

"So, you had *the talk*? Did she admit she loves you?"

"She wants to be more than friends," I conceded.

"That's the same as saying she loves you, Skyler," snarled my goddess. "If you can't tell she loves you, then you're an idiot. What did you say to her?"

"I said, 'Megan, you're a neat kid. I like you very much. I want to be friends, and nothing more,'" I summarized.

"Did she say anything about me?" Janeen's eyes narrowed.

"No. But I did," I took a deep breath and gathered my courage. "I told her the truth. I said, 'Janeen is The One. I'm in love with Janeen.'" My goddess betrayed no emotional reaction to my profession of love. I at least expected her to smile. We stood facing each other like two mannequins.

After a long pause, she asked, "How did Megan react?"

"She just said, 'Let's keep walking. It's a lovely night.'" I couldn't understand this line of questioning.

"Megan really does love you," Janeen sounded astonished. "She's a romantic; she must've thought that if you kept walking and holding hands, you might change your mind. Or that the mystical hemlock trees would do the trick!"

"I can't speak to Megan's thoughts. The meadow and woods were beautiful and quiet. We wanted to keep walking."

"What a perfectly romantic setting for you to reject her love," Janeen's voice dripped with sarcasm. "Did Megan cry?"

"Not that I'm aware of. Her eyes teared up from the frigid air once or twice," I described what I'd seen.

"Skyler, you're blind. Megan was heartbroken and disappointed." I didn't know what to say, so I stood there. Janeen asked again, "Did she say anything about me?" Unwilling to betray Megan's confidence, I paraphrased.

"She said, 'Janeen's great. If things don't work out between you two, I'll be waiting.'" The little cottage fell silent. I counted the ticking of the grandfather clock. Janeen meandered across the living room toward the picture window. She settled on the floor and pulled off her tall boots. I followed and sat beside her, unsure how to proceed or what to say. After a minute, she lay face down and stretched full-length on the area rug.

"Volleyball is wretched on my back. After that long drive, I need a back rub," it sounded like a cross between a command and a request, so I knelt perpendicular to her body with my knees touching her side. I began to massage her firm shoulder muscles. "Right there. That feels good," she sighed. "Sit on me and do my spine." I repositioned myself, taking deep breaths to calm my nerves as I rested my weight on her buttocks. "Press harder with your thumbs," she barked. I leaned forward and used all of my arm strength to dig in. "That's so good," she moaned. I developed a pattern starting at her shoulders, massaging down to her waist, and back up again.

"I must've hurt my lower back," she groaned after a few minutes passed. "Rub it, please." I moved my hands lower, spanning the area of her back below her waist to the top edge of her buttocks. I didn't dare extend my reach further without being invited. For an hour, my hands remained in continuous contact with her perfectly contoured frame. Slowly, I felt her relax. The tension in her back subsided. Even after I thought she'd fallen asleep, I kept massaging her. I watched her powerful back rise and fall under my hands. Every second was blissful. I wanted this massage to last all night. I wanted it to last the rest of my life.

"Do my hips. They're sore," Janeen's voice startled me. I inched the heels of my palms lower, then gently placed both hands on the sides of her hips, reluctant to push too hard. "That's not hard enough. Just lay on top of me and press down with your whole body," she sounded exasperated. I hurried to do as she asked. "Now, put all of your weight on my hips. Push down, keep the weight on me, then release. Do that again." I followed her instructions to the T as I mustered my courage to speak again.

"Janeen, I thought about your proposal. I love you. You're beautiful, inside and out. I want to marry you. I want to make you the happiest woman in the world. But I need to tell you—" before I could say another word, she rolled out from underneath me, and my butt landed on the floor with a thump. In one swoop, she whipped off her jacket and sweater. Her undershirt went, too, sticking to the sweater. Silently, she unclasped her bra and pitched it across the floor. Still speechless, I stared at her. She wrapped her arms around me and forced me onto my back. Her thigh pressed into my crotch, and I found myself pulled tight against her chest. As she kissed me, she sucked on my tongue. The memory of Kirsten threatened to intervene, but I refocused on my goddess. After kissing for a minute or two, Janeen flopped her back. She unbuckled her belt and unzipped her fly. Raising her bum, she shoved her jeans down to her thighs.

"Pull them off," she breathed. I sat up and grabbed one hem in each fist. She kicked her feet in the air so I could liberate her. "Away with my undies," she laughed and lifted her backside again. I tugged her panties over her muscular thighs. I was amazed by her beauty. "Give me those," she smiled licentiously. I tossed the panties on her naked torso. She snatched the slip of silk and lace, rolled it into a tiny ball, and threw it blindly down the hall toward my bedroom. "Keep 'em. My undies are your promissory note," she let out a belly laugh. "I can't believe I'm completely naked! I never do this with anyone," she pulled me down beside her. The next second, she grabbed my hands and placed one on either side of her face. "Touch me. I want a frontal massage. Go easy, please," she shut her eyes.

My fingers inched along her forehead and over her face. My thumb and forefinger stroked her neck and collarbone. Moving down her chest, my hands gently lingered on her small breasts. I continued teasing her taut flesh, making light circles on her stomach. My hand stopped and rested on her mons pubis. I could feel she was swollen and hot. Janeen arched her back, shoved her pelvis into my hand firmly, and moaned, "Enough already! The back rub turned me on plenty. I'm about to freaking explode. Take me!" Kirsten's specter hovered again.

"Let me get a condom," I managed to eke out.

"I can't wait! Just pull down your pants," her face, neck, and chest were blotched with red patches. She was the most beautiful woman I ever saw or touched, and I would follow her to the ends of the earth, doing her bidding. I unzipped my jeans and skinned them from my legs. I placed one hand on each of her gorgeous protruding hip bones. As if continuing the massage, I pressed gently on her hips. She bent her knees and spread her legs far apart, opening herself to me. Impulsively, I bent down to kiss her between the thighs. The tip of my tongue rolled up along her labia and touched her clitoris. She tasted moist and sweet.

"If you lick me again, I'll squirt all over your face," she moaned. "Now, before I cum, I need you inside me! Hurry!" I ripped off my sweater and shirt and crawled on top of my goddess. She guided me inside her, then grabbed my buttocks and pulled me deep within, arching her pelvis to meet mine. For a minute, we were entangled and immersed in each other. Then, she thrust up and down and screamed through her long volcanic orgasm. I came inside her. Feeling overwhelmed and blissful, I lay on top of her until her body cooled. Then, I rolled next to her. I pulled a blanket off the nearby sofa and draped it over us. She sat up when the grandfather clock tolled two in the morning.

"Aren't you going to say anything?" she asked.

"You're beautiful," I whispered.

"Yeah, right," she scoffed.

"You're welcome to spend the night. What's left of it, anyhow."

"I'm not staying overnight. After we're married, I'll move in."

"When, uh, how soon are we getting married?" I stuttered.

"After summer term. I'm thinking mid-August," she revealed her timeline.

"Janeen, if we wait until August, we won't be living in the cottage," I hesitated to correct her.

"Why not?" she looked puzzled.

"I tried to tell you; I haven't signed a new contract. And I won't. I can't work another year at the academy." My goddess's face went sheet white.

"You deceived me, you son of a bitch," she accused. "If you didn't sign your contract, why did you have...why did you touch me?"

"You asked for a back rub," I reminded her.

"Pick up my pants. Hand them to me right now," Janeen commanded, hostility rolling off her perfect body in waves. Feeling exposed in my naked state, I scrambled across the chilly floor and retrieved her jeans. She pulled them on.

"I need my sweater. What did you do with my sweater?" She looked around wildly, cupping her hands over her perfect breasts. I cast my eyes about the room. No sweater in sight. I spread my bare body on the frigid floor, reached under the couch, and found it.

"Give it here," Janeen barked. "Now, where's my shirt?" I looked everywhere, wanting to give her what she wanted, but the shirt was nowhere to be found. "Never mind! I don't care. I can't wait to get out of here," she yanked the sweater over her tousled hair, rolled up to standing, and went for her boots.

"Janeen, please calm down. Can we talk?" I found my clothes and turned them right-side out.

"No, never! I thought you were different, but you're just like every other man. What a disappointment. All you want is sex!"

"That's not true—"

"This is farewell, you bastard! Goodbye to you, forever," she flounced out of the cottage. Shocked, frustrated, and bewildered by what just happened, I stared at the front door for a long time before shutting off the lights and making my way to my bedroom.

CHAPTER 26
DILEMMA
SKYLER

The Next Day

S hortly after Janeen stormed out, I texted her.

> **Skyler**
> I'm sorry for the misunderstanding tonight.
>
> I care about you!
>
> Can we talk tomorrow?

She didn't reply. I went to bed, where I tossed and turned, replaying every word of our conversation, wishing I could have a do-over. I felt terrible about the way she left. I worried about her driving through the forest alone at night to her rental house in town. At least when she made it there, I told myself, she'd have Megan nearby to console her. Finally, I slept.

When I woke, my first thought was of my goddess. Fortunately, or perhaps unfortunately, the majority of the academy students were still enjoying the break off-campus. Other staff members were scheduled to oversee the activities of the day, leaving me with too much time to think. All morning, I was dysfunctional. I couldn't eat. I couldn't move. I desperately wanted to speak with Janeen.

At noon, I finally received a reply to my text message.

Janeen
I do not want to see you.

Don't bother me.

For hours, I sat at the kitchen table in my lonely cottage and tormented myself with endless questions. Would Janeen ever see me again? If she refused to talk to me, how could I restore our relationship? What if she told Megan everything, and Megan didn't want anything to do with me, either? Late in the afternoon, I drove to the tiny house the girls rented. I knocked several times before Megan cracked the door.

"Skyler, I'm surprised to see you," she said. "Are you here for Janeen or me?"

"While I enjoy talking with you, Megan, today I stopped to see Janeen," I answered sheepishly.

"Janeen's not available at the moment," she crossed her arms.

"Can you please tell her I'm here? I need to speak with her. It's urgent."

"She's sleeping. She's been sick all day," Megan reached out to shut the door. Before she did, she promised, "I'll tell her you came by." At least I knew Janeen arrived home safely.

To delay returning to my empty cottage, I drove further into town. I felt weak; I knew I had to eat. I made my way to one of my favorite greasy spoons and ordered a bowl of Hungarian Goulash. I barely tasted it. All I could think was, *I'm alone. Again.*

CHAPTER 27
CONFRONTATION
GRADY

Ten Days Later

One bright winter's afternoon a week into the second semester, I lingered in my office, waiting on Skyler. He'd requested an appointment on short notice, naming no subject. While I waited, I broke out my new putter. For Christmas, my wife surprised me with an AstroTurf office green. Come summer, my short game would be the envy of the Frat Row Foursome. As I tapped ball after ball in with practiced precision, I mulled over the state of the academy and the stellar admin team I'd assembled.

Everything was coming up aces. The volleyball pavilion was well underway, thanks to good ol' Don greasing the works. Amber ran a tight disciplinary ship; tardies and detentions declined year-over-year, and no new rivalries developed between cliques in the first semester. Megan was halfway done modernizing the academy's course curriculum in preparation for welcoming boys to campus next year. Janeen was...well, she was Janeen! I patted myself on the back for bagging such a brilliant hire. Skyler, my heir apparent, worked daily miracles managing the construction and outfitting of the new boys' dormitory. I sank a tricky shot, thinking, *damn, I'm proud of the professional he's become under my wing!*

The devil knocked politely on my office door.

"Don't be shy, my boy," I waved him in, keeping my stance. "Everything smoothed over with the landscape architect?" I studied the lay of my final putt.

"Yes. Before Independence Day, they'll finish terraforming and planting beds around the new building. The ground cover will be mature enough to overwinter," Skyler shifted his weight uncomfortably from foot to foot while he waited for me to take my stroke. I did. The ball skirted the edge of the cup.

"Have a seat and tell me what's on your mind, son," I went to retrieve the wayward golf ball. Skyler sat and cleared his throat several times before getting to the point.

"Grady, serving at the academy has been a privilege. I believe I've accomplished a great deal as a member of your team. I hope you agree. For the rest of my life, I'll be indebted to you," as he delivered his speech, it hit me where this conversation was headed. "However, it's time for me to move on with my career. I'm submitting my resignation."

"I don't accept," I said calmly. He blinked. Chuckling to myself, I thought, *you still have much to learn, young grasshopper.* "Best admit you don't have the upper hand in this negotiation, my boy. I know you love your job. You should; you're good at it. I also know you love this academy as much as I do. Your resignation doesn't make sense."

"I loved working here, and I loved working with you. I gave my heart to this school and its residents."

"What will you be if you're not Big Skyler's right-hand man?" I chipped at his ego. "Sure, your reputation is spreading, but you're still a toddler compared to the big boys in our industry."

"I'm not looking to move to another job, Grady. I plan to get a master's degree to advance my career," his poker face held steady.

"Nice try, my boy, but lest you forget, I taught you everything you know. Now, tell me what you're really thinking." He stared at me silently. Little Skyler had indeed become a shrewd bargainer. "If this is your way of asking for a raise, I'll give you ten percent, effective immediately. Sign the contract today, and you'll also receive a one-time bonus equivalent to one month's salary."

"I appreciate that. However, it's not about the money."

"If I've told you once, I've told you a thousand times. It's *always* about money," I sighed. The cheeky bastard said nothing. "Fine. If you need more persuasion, I'll tack on a guaranteed five percent above whatever the Board approves for your subsequent contract," I sweetened the pot.

"The truth is that I've already accomplished the goals I set for myself at the academy. I proved myself. I'm sorry, but there's no future for me here," he didn't seem about to budge.

"Why not stay where you have seniority, and know the drill? Your career will grow in time, my boy. One day, you'll take my place as Executive Director. The Board already drafted the succession plan," I enticed him with top-secret information.

"I respect you, and I admire all you do for the academy, Grady. Unfortunately, I can't say that's my career goal," at least he had the good grace to look a little guilty at his betrayal.

"Is this about your generation's obsession with so-called work-life balance? If it is, I can tell you I submitted a request to the Board to hire a second assistant for you. Once that person's on board, you'll have one week's vacation per month in the summer, a week off during winter break, and your on-call duties will be halved. It's not in the budget for next school year, but soon."

"I've made my decision, Grady. I need to move on with my life," Skyler rejected the bounty I'd laid at his feet.

I snapped, "Didn't your mother teach you manners? I stuck my neck out advocating with the Board for all these upgrades to your position!"

"I'm sorry I upset you. I appreciate everything you did, even though I won't benefit from it." This conversation was not going the way I wanted. I wondered when my apprentice became so unmanageable.

"Once you leave the academy, your career will be finished," I pronounced. "Face it, Skyler, you're nothing without me propping you up."

"Do you want me to leave immediately?" he asked mildly.

"After I hire your replacement, you can train them. Then you'll be free to go."

Wordlessly, Skyler stood up and walked out of my office. I slammed the door behind him.

CHAPTER 28
COMMITMENTS
JANEEN

Valentine's Day

D awdling in my bedroom while getting ready for work, a knock at the front door alarmed me. I threw on my robe and wondered what kind of Neanderthal would stop by before seven. I squinted out the peephole. Looked like a delivery man, but you could never be sure.

Through the closed door, I shouted, "What are you doing here?"

"Looking for Janeen. Is this the right address?"

"What do you want with her?"

"Flower delivery. Can you please sign?"

"Leave it on the porch," I called.

"No, ma'am. It's my ass if they freeze and die out here. Someone has to sign." Reluctantly, I unbolted and unchained the door but kept my foot against it as a backstop in case this guy tried to lunge through.

"There's been a mistake. No one sends me flowers."

"Well, then, it's your lucky day. Someone mistakenly sent you roses. Sign here," he held out an electronic pad.

After locking the door behind him, I lugged a massive lead-glass vase stuffed with two dozen long-stemmed red roses, clouds of baby's breath, and trailing lacy-green ferns to the kitchen table. The gaudy display, encircled with a giant white velvet bow, made a brilliant splash of color on a bleak midwinter's day. Inhaling the sweet fragrance, I had to admit I felt pampered and adored. I reached between blossoms and thorns to retrieve the card.

To Janeen, with love always. Yours, Skyler.

A pang of guilt hit me. This gift cost a fortune! Not for the first time, I wondered if I'd judged him too harshly after our blow-up following winter break. Maybe he'd reconsidered his ill-advised decision to ditch me and was ready to sign a new contract at the academy.

Conscious that Megan likely still felt the sting of Skyler's rejection, I carried the bouquet to my bedroom. No point in bringing up hurt feelings by leaving them where she'd have to stare at them every time she departed or came home. After arranging the vase on my dresser and fiddling with a few of the blooms so I could see them better, I texted Skyler.

Janeen
Roses received, thank you!

See you at 10 tonight at your place.

Skyler
Okay, see you then.

I spent the entire day thinking about him, which wasn't new. There'd been more than a few days since I stormed out of his cottage when I wished I could go back and smooth things over. Though I'd accused Skyler of being like other men, I realized after the fact that wasn't the case. He'd politely given me space for the past six weeks. He watched me when he thought I wasn't looking, but I knew. If I was seated in the dining hall when he arrived, he maintained a respectful distance, smiling tentatively when our eyes met but not demanding my attention. During Grady's weekly staff meetings and whenever we had to work together for our jobs, he was always professional and betrayed no signs of resentment. Maybe tonight, he'd be ready to come to terms and get back together.

THAT NIGHT, WHEN SKYLER LET ME INTO HIS COTTAGE, I stood in the living room staring at him. He waited for me to speak first.

"Did you change your mind about staying at the academy?" I asked bluntly.

"I'm torn," he sounded miserable. "I want a relationship with you. But I need room to grow in my career. And I can't work for Grady any longer." I wasn't willing to wait around while he hemmed and hawed.

"Well, it's go-time. What's your final decision?" It took him a couple of minutes to answer.

"I'm sorry, Janeen. My decision's made. The academy and I are finished. Work this year felt like trudging through an endless, dark tunnel," he started making excuses. "There were days when I struggled to accomplish anything; I felt so apathetic. The only time I was happy was hanging out with you and Megan."

"If we got married, if I lived in this cottage with you, wouldn't that renew your enthusiasm?"

"I want to marry you; believe me, I do," he looked yearning and sad. "But I don't want to live out my life here. It's time for me to move on."

"Well, what about us? Are you moving on from me?"

"I love you. I'll never love another woman the way I love you. You're the one that I want. Unfortunately, the time and the place are terrible."

"Stop talking," I marched down the hall to his bedroom, where I tossed my jacket in the corner. I yanked off my boots and threw them across the room. They bounded against the wall, leaving a dirty mark. I sat on his bed and pulled my sweater over my head. As I unzipped my jeans, Skyler finally walked in.

"What are you—" he started to ask.

"Don't say a word," I cut him off. He stood by the door with a mystified look on his face. "Come here." As he approached, I kicked off my pants. "Take off your clothes on the way," I ordered. Without hesitating, Skyler began to undress. I stood to draw back the bed quilt, then lay on my back watching him.

"Are you sure about this?" he said when he was naked. "I don't want to do it if there'll be regrets." I crooked my finger at him, and he joined me on the bed. Lying beside me, he ran his fingers gently over my neck, shoulders, breasts, and belly. His teasing feathery touch drove me mad. When I couldn't take any more, I grabbed his shoulders and dragged him on top of me. We kissed passionately before his lips wandered lower to my jawline and nipples.

"I want you inside of me," I whispered. Without waiting for him to agree, I spread my legs, and he slipped in. I was extremely wet. The sex didn't last long. As I climaxed, I nearly bucked him off. Afterward, we held each other for a long time. Eventually, Skyler spoke.

"To stay close to you, I'm willing to find a job nearby," he said. It hurt my heart to hear him sound so unhappy.

"No," I shook my head. "You said so yourself; you need to move on with your life. I won't stand in your way."

"Come with me," he offered, excitement brightening his tone. "If you can't leave tomorrow, wait until I start graduate school and join me."

"I'm staying at the academy, Skyler," I tried to let him down gently. "This is where I belong right now. Besides, I want to be close to my sister. She's my forever friend," I set my boundaries.

"But you won't stay at the academy forever, will you?"

"Most likely, I'll work here for a short time. The compensation package Grady gave me is ridiculously generous, and the national exposure I've already gotten guarantees I'll be able to write my own ticket wherever I go next."

"Then, take advantage of that. Resign at the end of the term and come to me. We'll figure out where you want to work, and I'll go to grad school nearby," he pleaded.

"That's not happening, Skyler," I was getting exasperated. "Stop fantasizing about us! I know one thing. I'm not going to see you again. Our time has passed," I stood up and started looking for my clothes. "Go to graduate school. Make something of yourself."

Those were the last words I spoke to Skyler. We dressed silently. By the front door, we hugged. I walked out of the cottage. Without looking back, I made my way to my car and drove home.

The next day, I was shocked when Grady came to my office in the gym to deliver the news. Skyler had indeed moved forward without me. I hadn't realized he meant he was literally departing *the next day* when he invited me to leave tomorrow!

After Grady bustled off to share the news with someone else, I caught sight of Skyler's car slowly proceeding down the long academy driveway. From my office window, I could see that he kept turning his head, looking at the gymnasium.

CHAPTER 29
REGRETS
JANEEN

March

The day after Skyler left the academy, he messaged me.

Skyler
You're the best. Love you always!

I didn't respond. The next day, he tried to call twice. I didn't answer. Late at night, he texted again.

Skyler
Arrived at my destination safely.

I deleted it without replying. I figured that would be the end of our communication. Beginning a week later, I received a text and a phone call from Skyler nearly every day. He never left a voicemail, but his texts revealed the range of emotions swirling in their author's heart.

Skyler
How are you?

It was an innocent enough question, but I could tell he was in denial.

Skyler
Can't believe how much I miss you.

The depression must be setting in.

Skyler
Remember, I'll always love you.

That one sounded like acceptance. I hoped to receive nothing further. But soon after, he was in the bargaining phase.

Skyler
Please, let's get back together! I treasure you, and I'll do whatever it takes to make you happy.

I liked that one least of all. What would have made me happy was his staying at the academy when I asked him to. But that crossroads was behind us now. After about ten days of one-sided conversation, he sent another question.

Skyler
Are you receiving my text messages?

I maintained my silence, praying he'd give up. Two

weeks passed with no contact. Things started to feel normal again as I got into the swing of the spring sports season. Then, a little over a month after he drove off, I was surprised to receive an old-fashioned letter from him.

Dear Janeen,

I hope you're well. What's new at the academy? How are your teams shaping up? I bet the girls are enjoying the new volleyball pavilion and are excited about the sand pits. I wish I could be there when they open.

I found a new job working at a treatment center. While it's a residential program, the staff doesn't live on campus. Working from nine to five, Monday through Friday, is different for me. I'm adjusting to having free time and trying to make friends. I've already been accepted into a graduate program. Classes start in the fall. My employer will accommodate my school schedule.

I miss you. I miss your explosive laughter. I miss your smile. I miss looking into your jet-black eyes. I miss the scent of your hair. I miss touching every inch of your fabulous body. I miss your heart and soul. Most of all, I miss your presence. I want you to move here and live with me. If you wish, we can get married. I would be honored to marry you.

Please visit me over the summer so we can discuss our plans face-to-face. Please answer my phone calls. Please reply to my texts. Please respond to this letter.

Love always,
Skyler

That night, I crept into Megan's bedroom while she slept. I climbed into her bed and snuggled next to her. She turned, smiled sleepily, and wrapped her arms and legs around me. Wordlessly, she fell into a deep slumber. As she breathed, I felt Megan's heart beating. She was warm. I got hot. With her body tightly twisted around mine, I couldn't move. Lying there sleepless, I meditated on Skyler's letter. It had grown increasingly clear that he cared for me deeply, and his letter was proof. I wondered if I should respond. I missed him more than I'd believed it possible to miss any man. *But then,* I reminded myself, *Skyler isn't just any man.*

I recalled the two times we made love, reliving the moments in my mind without moving a muscle in the cocoon of Megan's embrace. To put it mildly, my sexual experiences before Skyler had been less than enjoyable. But I loved his touch, craved it, even. What if I never found anyone else I could have such uninhibited sex with? I never believed that sex was so important until I felt what it could be with Skyler. *Maybe he's the love of my life,* I thought. *Maybe he's my soulmate.*

I lay awake when the day dawned, still contemplating the future of our relationship. Megan stretched and hugged me tight when she woke. She hopped out of bed to make us a breakfast of sausage, eggs, and pancakes. I followed her, watching silently while she bustled around the kitchen.

When we sat to eat, she said, "Janeen, we've got to talk about last night." I swallowed and nodded nervously. "What's happening between us?" she asked. I couldn't find my tongue, so she offered, "I'll go first. I'm not afraid to tell you about my feelings. I'm deeply attracted to you. I love you," she watched my face closely. "I'm not sure I'm a lesbian; labels don't mean much to me. I do know that tonight, I want you to crawl in bed with me again."

"I like living with you, Megan. You make me feel safe. I need you," I tried to be as truthful and straightforward as possible. I didn't want to lead her on in any way.

"What about Skyler? We never talked about what happened between the three of us. Everything changed over winter break, and then he disappeared practically without a word."

"He and I sort of got together," I admitted. "Then we broke up, and I warned him to stay away. I'm sorry I hid all of that from you. I saw you were confused. But I was afraid to say anything because we both liked him. I didn't want to hurt you."

"I understand," she reached across the table to take my hand. "Both of you have a hard time displaying your emotions. You could've knocked me over with a feather when Skyler told me he loved you on New Year's Eve after I made a pass at him," she laughed good-naturedly. "I hoped you'd eventually feel like you could confide in me, too. I'm glad that moment is here. My curiosity has been in overdrive for two months." Relief flooded me. Megan wasn't hurt or upset. She wanted to talk, and I needed a shoulder to lean on. Colette tended to be overprotective, so I hadn't shared the full extent of Skyler's and my relationship with her.

"I got a letter from Skyler yesterday. He already landed a new job, and he's starting his master's degree in the fall. He invited me to visit next summer so we can talk about moving in together and getting married."

"Are you going to go?" Megan asked eagerly.

"No," I shook my head, deciding my course of action. "I gave myself to him in a way I've never given myself to anyone. He rejected me. I'm not interested in rekindling the relationship."

"Are you sure? Skyler loves you, Janeen."

"My feelings for Skyler were wrapped up with life at the academy. When he quit and drove away, all of that came undone. It's over," I said.

"You had a crazy intense connection," Megan advised. "You may want to take some time to reconsider. If you want to go to him, I'll understand."

"My decision's been made, Megan. I like where I am. I belong here."

CHAPTER 30
ADMONISHMENT
FRANCINE

May

"It's about time you decided to pay your mother a visit," I swung open the massive front door. Rainbow flecks wheeled around the foyer, refracting through the leaded crystal glass sunburst.

"Hello, Mother. Nice to see you, too," Skyler said.

"You moved to the city two months ago. Why couldn't you stop to see me sooner?" I stepped back to allow him to enter.

"I've been busy getting settled," he started making excuses.

"Well, now that you're nearby, I expect you to have coffee with me every Saturday morning," I shut the door, then led him into the kitchen where we sat on opposite ends of the breakfast table. "And Sunday dinner with me each week."

"Neither of those is happening," Skyler shook his head. "We get along just fine seeing each other once a year."

"You're my only child, Skyler. I want you to spend time with me."

"I'm not here to be suffocated."

"I gave up so much for you," maybe a reminder of my sacrifices in his name would have the desired effect. "My divorce from your father is your fault, you know. I had to move here with you so you could go to the prep school that got you into your beloved university. The least you could do is respect my wishes." Skyler sat silent as a stone. "All of my friends' children spend time with them. Remember Kirsten Jones? She and her husband spend every weekend at Alyssa's house with their kids. Kirsten has the proper Christian ideas of duty and family responsibility."

"I'm glad for Mrs. Jones that she gets to spend time with her grandkids," said Skyler. "But that doesn't change my plans."

"Well, I know it didn't take you two months to move in. What else were you doing that was more important than seeing your mother?"

"I got accepted to graduate school, and I got a part-time job."

"*Graduate school?*" I didn't even try to mask my agitation. "You should work in business. That's what our family does. Look at your father. Look at me. I'm going to set up a job interview for you at my company."

"No, thank you. I'm working at a residential treatment center. To move forward with my career, I need a master's degree in social work, public administration, or finance."

"You quit working at the academy?" I was shocked. Skyler only talked about three things: the academy, the students, and the endless projects he undertook for the low-class buffoon boss I hoped never to meet.

"Yes. No more 24 hours a day 365 days a year. I need a life outside work."

"You should start doing something respectable. Make a real contribution to the world. Social work? Public health? Those aren't suitable jobs for a man, Skyler. You're drifting and wasting your time," I tried to talk sense to him.

"I think, in my own small way, I'm making a difference in the world. I'm trying to change the system and improve people's lives." I winced. *He's weak and soft,* I thought to myself.

"Why didn't you ask to move home?" I changed the subject. "Why would you rather live in a strange city where no one knows you?"

"I'm not moving back into your house, Mother."

"I only want what's best for you. You need my encouragement to make good choices," again, I tried to reason with him.

"I'm never living with you again. Period. End of discussion," he said with surprising firmness. I sipped my coffee.

"Where are you living?"

"Sixty-five miles north of here. I'm moving into a cottage along the big lake."

"You can't afford to live along the lakeshore. Certainly not as a graduate student. And never as a social worker. The least expensive home costs over a million dollars. Are you on the water or near the water?"

"On the water," his calm smile irked me.

"How are you paying rent?"

"I found a roommate," he refused to look me in the eye.

"Who's your roommate?"

"I prefer not to tell you, and trust me, you'd prefer not to know. I want us to be able to get along," he blushed.

"I demand to know who you're living with, Skyler. If for no other reason than for your safety," I watched him debate in his head. I leaned in and pressed my advantage. "What if something happens and I can't reach you? I need to know whom to contact."

"Fine. Since you insist, I'll tell you, but you're not going to like it. My roommate is Chelsea." I felt the blood leave my face.

"Chelsea? As in, Chelsea, the school tramp?" Skyler nodded. "What are you thinking, Skyler? This is abominable! I won't have it!" I found myself yelling.

"I'm old enough to make my own decisions, Mother. I've lived independently for nearly a decade!" Skyler's voice rose to meet mine.

"Are you simply sharing expenses, or are you involved with *that girl?*" I struggled to ask the next question. "Are you sleeping with her?"

"That's not your business," he snapped.

"Everything you do is my business. You're my son! Your behavior is a direct reflection on me."

"I'm sorry that my image fails to meet your standards, Mother," Skyler sat back, and his tone cooled. "I didn't date in high school. I didn't have a girlfriend in college. I lived a celibate life at the academy. I'm not waiting any longer. If I want to live with a beautiful woman, I will." I stared at him. "You should be happy for me. Chelsea is good for me."

"You don't want to hear what I've got to say, but I'm going to say it anyway because someone must point out your wrongheadedness. You should *not* be living with Chelsea. Not only is it flaunting one of God's commandments, but she's not our kind. You can do so much better, Skyler.

Chelsea may be out of poverty. She may even be wealthy. But mark my words; in time, her baggage will be an albatross around your neck," I warned.

"Chelsea changed, Mother. Her head is on straight. She's a survivor, and she's had years of therapy. Now, she has a great career. She works in the tech field. Makes tons of money. But do you know what? Even if she weren't so successful, I'd still like her. She's my one true friend."

"Good for you," I sneered. "However, I'm not changing my mind about *that girl*. I don't want you involved with her. I don't want her to be part of our lives, even on the outskirts. Lord, I pray you're not sleeping with her! I don't want you getting her pregnant. I don't want her to be the mother of my grandchildren," I railed at my ungrateful, pigheaded, misguided son. "Do not bring her to my house. Ever!" Skyler stood up and pushed his chair in.

"The extent of my involvement with Chelsea is my business. Not yours," he turned, walked away, and slammed the front door behind him.

CHAPTER 31
REUNION
CHELSEA

The Next Day

My mind wandered over my afternoon agenda as I washed and put away my brunch dishes. An important conversation with Skyler loomed. When he called two weeks ago, I was shocked to learn that he'd quit his beloved academy, moved here, found a new job, and been accepted to grad school all since the beginning of the year. He never told me about any of it while it was happening. After his revelations, we met and got reacquainted. I showed him my favorite haunts around town and introduced him to the few friends I enjoyed spending time with. We talked on the phone every evening for hours, rekindling our old connection.

Eventually, the truth came out about Janeen's proposal and their subsequent falling out. He asked if he could live with me for a few months. I tentatively agreed, pending a tour of my new lakefront cottage and a discussion of ground rules. Today was the day for us to hammer out the details of our agreement. He knocked.

"Come in, Skyler! The door's open," I yelled, walking from the chef's kitchen to meet him in the foyer. We hugged, and I said, "Let me show you why I chose this place. The entire back wall of the cottage is windows," I took him on the grand tour, pausing to show him the panoramic scene overlooking the lake to the west of the house. "Can you believe this view?"

"Amazing," he said appreciatively. "The sunsets must be incredible."

"Exactly. It's instant stress relief."

"Where will I be staying?"

"As I told you, this place is big, but it's only got one bedroom that we'll share. I bought a second dresser. You can have half of the closet, too. It's a walk-in," I showed him everything before we headed back downstairs and into the cavernous kitchen. "We'll split grocery expenses fifty-fifty," I said matter-of-factly. "And there are a few other details we need to set straight."

"Yes, let's be open and honest," Skyler nodded.

"I'm glad you feel that way. It's the only option for me," I smiled. "Please make yourself at home. But remember, this is my house. Understood?"

"Yes, Lady Chelsea," he bowed. I was happy he was in a playful mood, but it was poorly timed. Boundaries were super important to me. I hoped we could have a serious heart-to-heart and reach a healthy agreement to cohabitate.

"Let's go outside. I want to show you another reason I love it here," I grabbed a plaid woolen blanket that was folded over the back of a rocking chair and led him out the back door. We paused after walking a short distance north along the sandy ridge where the cottage stood. A broad expanse of dunes spread further north, and a dusky forest loomed in the middle distance.

Skyler pointed and exclaimed, "Hemlock trees!"

"They were a sign," I nodded, thrilled he identified them so quickly. "Once I saw them, I knew I needed to buy this cottage. Walk with me. I want to sit under the hemlock trees as we did in high school. We have more to talk about."

"Is it okay if I grab something from my car first?"

"Sure, I'll wait here." He trotted back the way we came and out of sight around the cottage. I folded my arms over my chest, gazing westward across the calm lake waters while I waited. I loved the feeling of knowing my friend was here and we would spend time together. Skyler rejoined me after a few minutes with his backpack slung over his shoulders.

"I'm ready," he announced. "Lead the way, my lady!"

"What's in the bag?" I was intrigued.

"You'll have to wait and see," he smiled mysteriously. "I've held onto it for years." We started north across the dunes, soon arriving at the shady edge of the hemlock forest. "Oh, the memories," the same dreamy, appreciative look I recalled from high school stole over Skyler's face when we stepped under the evergreen canopy. I took his hand in mine.

"Are you sure you're ready to live with me?" I asked as we picked our way between massive trunks.

"Yes, of course. You're my best friend in the world, and I love you. I feel safe with you."

"Are you okay with us living openly together while not married?"

"I want to be with you if that's what you're asking," he glanced sideways at me.

"That's not what I'm asking. I want you to check in

with yourself and be sure you're okay with our arrangement, given your beliefs and your religious identity," I
explained.

"You know me well," he looked thoughtful. "I believe in
the Providence of God. I believe He wants us to find happiness and peace on Earth. Our arrangement makes me
happy. It gives me peace."

"I'm glad to hear that."

"Since I left the academy, I've been attending church on
Sundays. You're welcome to join me."

"Thanks, but that's unlikely. I believe in a higher power,
yet I haven't set foot in a church in years. Christians badly
burned me."

"I remember," he nodded. "I've done some recovery
work myself. I'm learning to forgive and let go of the things I
can't control. I decided not to let any so-called Christians
from my past rob me of my relationship with our Heavenly
Father."

"That's wonderful, Skyler," I was relieved to hear that
his approach to religion had moderated over the years. "I
don't want to stand in your way. I want you to explore your
faith."

"I prefer the word spirituality," he smiled serenely.

"I've been doing some spiritual work, too. I'm taking
yoga, tai chi, and meditation classes at the YMCA downtown. It's helped me let go of the past."

"I'm happy for you, Chelsea," Skyler squeezed my
hand. "After my academy implosion, I finally started jour-
naling. Remember in the enchanted forest, we agreed to
keep a journal while we were separated? Getting my
thoughts out on paper has been a welcome form of self-
care."

"Oh, I'd forgotten," I smiled at the memory of our

wistful parting a decade ago. "I have a stack of journals I've filled up over the years."

"I can't wait to show you what's in my backpack. You'll never guess what it is," he grinned mischievously.

"Animal, vegetable, or mineral?"

"You'll have to wait and see," he repeated. The shadows under the hemlocks grew darker the further we wended into the lakeside forest.

"I've been working with a personal trainer. Can you tell?" I turned to show off my profile. I was proud of the way I'd sculpted my curvy body. I felt strong and confident.

"I always liked the way you looked," Skyler reminded me.

I laughed appreciatively, "I know you did! You were the only one in high school who accepted me. I've always loved you for that."

"I confess, I always thought you were sexy. And now you're a little hottie," Skyler flirted.

"Shut up, liar. I'm not a hottie," I playfully bumped his shoulder with mine. Deep down, I loved the affirmation. We walked in silence for a moment. "I want to keep working on ground rules, Skyler. If our relationship turns sour, you'll be leaving. There'll be no negotiating or do-overs. Do you agree?"

"Fair enough," he said.

"Unless something changes and we make a new agreement, living with me is not a long-term thing. I'd like us to agree to a six-month trial period. We can renegotiate in the fall."

"I want a long-term relationship with you, but I accept your parameters," he acquiesced after a few moments' silence. "I plan to move into graduate housing on campus in the fall."

So far, so good, I thought. I took a deep breath. It was time to talk about the intimate aspects of our arrangement. This was the part of the discussion I had my doubts about. I knew Skyler was still immature in his approach to romantic relationships. That had become clear to me as we discussed the Janeen and Megan situation and how he handled the fallout.

"Can we talk about sex?" I asked bluntly.

"Yes," he blushed.

"I told you I've spent a lot of time in therapy under-standing what went wrong with my childhood and teenage years. I was used and sexually abused. I retaliated. I used sex in unhealthy ways. I view it differently these days," I watched him closely. He was listening, but I could tell he didn't know how to react or carry the conversation. "I slept with more men and women than you can ever imagine. I need you to be honest with me about sex. If you want to have sex, ask. Use your words. I'll do the same."

"Okay." I hoped for a more in-depth response but was willing to give him time to digest.

"During sex, I'll tell you if something doesn't feel right. No offense should be taken; we all have different comfort levels. I expect you to do the same. My safe words are 'no,' 'stop,' and 'get off me.' That means, whatever the hell you're doing, stop immediately."

"I understand. I'll try to satisfy you," Skyler said. Again, I wasn't sure we were speaking on the same level, but I wanted this to work. I was willing to coach him to a certain degree.

"No, thank you," I said firmly. "I'll satisfy myself. You satisfy yourself. Be real. Communicate."

"Communication is something I've been working on," he looked self-conscious. "I'll do my best."

"That's a start," I nodded. "Let's talk about feelings. We're partners with benefits. Lovers, but not in love. Are you okay with this description of our relationship?"

"Sure."

"Good. Now, I'm into serial monogamy. If you're going to have sex with someone else, you need to tell me. Ideally, before you fuck them. This applies to men as well as women. If you want to experiment with others, that's fine, but our physical relationship will end. I'll need your promise."

"Okay, yes, you have my word," he stammered and turned deep red. I wondered if I was taking too big a risk. Holding space for him while he figured out how to get comfortable with the frank adult talk was one thing; being his sex therapist was another.

"This includes Janeen," I emphasized. "If you even start thinking about getting back together with her, I need to know."

"Chelsea, I told you that's over. Janeen never responded to my texts, calls, or my letter. For what it's worth, I only slept with her once in January and once in February."

"Skyler, I can tell you're still in love with her. I'm okay with that. I'm just asking you to make a simple commitment to decency. I get that Janeen is your unicorn, so I want this to be acknowledged upfront. This is what a healthy relationship with shared boundaries and communication looks like."

Skyler nodded, saying, "I promise to be transparent and forthcoming about Janeen."

"Thank you. That's everything from my side. What rules do you need to feel safe in our connection?"

"You could write a how-to book about sexuality and healthy relationships," he laughed nervously.

"Funny you should say that. You remember my high school experiences, don't you? Wham, bam, thank you, ma'am," I had to smile at the memories. Even the painful ones had mellowed as I processed my emotions and matured. "I'm definitely going to publish a tell-all someday. You're in a small chapter. Stick around, and you may get two." We laughed companionably. My spirits rose; maybe this would be a mutually beneficial, grown-up relationship after all.

A few minutes later, we reached our destination. We paused under a hemlock giant; it wasn't as huge as the one in our enchanted forest back home, but it was magnificent nonetheless.

"Wow," Skyler breathed. "It's like going back in time." I spread the blanket out for us to sit under the hemlock tree while he shrugged off his backpack and unzipped it. "I hope you won't be angry," he said. "I have something of yours."

"Something of mine? I never gave you anything," I was perplexed.

"Let me explain. I was lost without you after you moved in the middle of our senior year. One cold winter day, I felt compelled to visit your old house. Stepping inside, I felt your presence. I made my way upstairs, following your strawberry fragrance. I sensed your spirit lingering in the attic bedroom," he turned around, reached into his backpack, pulled out an old cardboard shoe box, and handed it to me. "Here, these belong to you."

When I opened the lid, I found my tattered, half-naked antique doll, a sweater my mom had knitted for me eons ago, and my long-lost childhood journal. I drew the box to my chest.

"All these years, you've kept my journal? And my little

dolly?" Tears swelled in my eyes. I couldn't contain myself; I wept. Skyler waited to speak until the storm passed.

"Every day after I found them until I moved away to college, I read your journal. I treasured each word. I hope you're not upset," he said quietly.

"I'm grateful and touched," I wiped my eyes and sniffled. "My sweater, too, how precious. My mother made it. I loved it. Green was my favorite color. Thank you," my heart raced. I leaned forward and kissed his forehead.

"I'm glad you're not mad at me. I always intended to return the mementos of your past, or rather of my obsession with you," he smiled tentatively. I set aside the memorabilia.

"Come here, Skyler," I crooked my finger at him and shot him a come-hither look. "What do you say we practice our safe signals?" The old fear dawned in his eyes. He started to slither backward but quickly changed his mind and leaned in to kiss me. I pulled back after a dizzying embrace. "Before dinner, I want a snack," I raised my eyebrows at him. He grinned devilishly. "Let me show you the joy to be found under the hemlock trees."

The End

ABOUT THE AUTHOR

Aubrey DeLacette is a life-long champion for social and emotional development in adolescents and young adults. In service of these values, prior to becoming an author, Aubrey worked as a health professional in educational, community, and clinical settings. Aubrey held state, national, and international credentials in the promotion of reproductive health, mental health, wellness, and the prevention of substance abuse and suicide.

Under the Hemlock Tree presents a fictional account of adolescents and young adults struggling to develop their identities, relationships, and sexuality while managing common 21st Century societal and family pressures of isolation, abandonment, and abuse. While the story and characters are fictional, Aubrey DeLacette exposes the impact of familiar traumatic experiences on young men and women by drawing on a wealth of personal experience and professional knowledge.